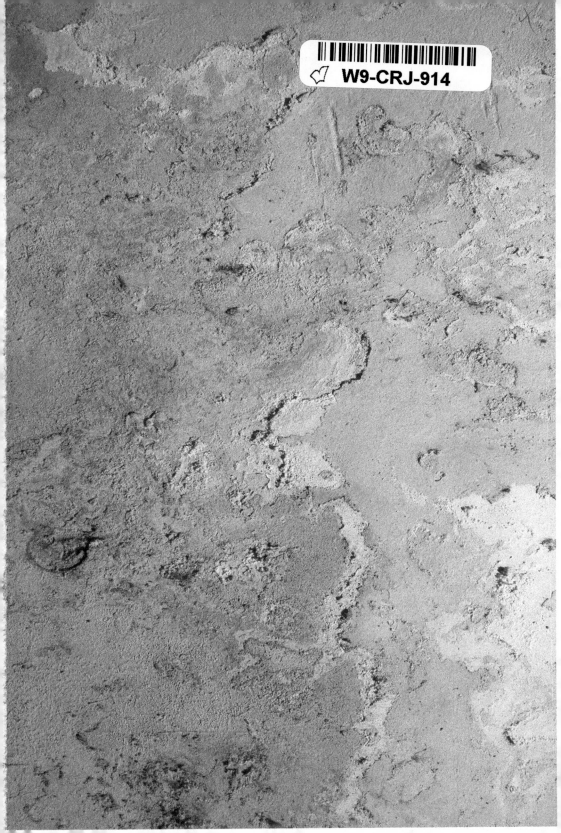

Praise for Eric LaRocca and *We Can Never Leave This Place*

"*We Can Never Leave This Place* is the apocalyptic 21st century Grimm's fairy tale you need in your life. Eric LaRocca plucks images directly from the muck and mire of our id and fashions them into something grotesquely beautiful." ~ Paul Tremblay, author of *The Cabin at the End of the World* and *The Pallbearers Club*

"*We Can Never Leave This Place* is a bleak and tender, monstrous and visceral fable of family and loss, and the courage it takes to confront them both." ~ Kathe Koja, author of *The Cipher*

"*We Can Never Leave This Place* is bleak, desolate Gothic horror at its best. A hateful fairytale populated by the most disgusting human-sized insects to grace the page since Gregor Samsa awoke from his troubled dreams." ~ Gretchen Felker-Martin, author of *Manhunt*

"*We Can Never Leave This Place* fulfills the promise of LaRocca's previous work, presenting an unflinchingly grisly vision of rage, grief, and sacrifice during an unnamed war in an unnamed city in an unnamed country. Very few stories leave you bruised as you confront each page, and this is firmly nestled within that rarefied company." ~ David Demchuk, author of *Red X* and *The Bone Mother*

"There's something wrong with Eric LaRocca, and I mean that in the very best way possible. His stories stick a screw right into your heart-meat. Looking forward to whatever gut-clenching horror he has coming." ~ Chuck Wendig, New York Times best-selling author of *The Book of Accidents*

"LaRocca proves that the sickest minds can have the biggest hearts – he's a twisted, tender new talent." ~ Daniel Kraus, New York Times best-selling author of *The Living Dead*

"Eric LaRocca is truly original, truly subversive, and truly talented." ~ Priya Sharma, author of *Ormeshadow*

"With an Eric LaRocca story, you never know what you're getting into. And I say that with admiration... Blazing creativity meets ferocious writing." ~ Jonathan Janz, author of *The Raven* and *The Siren and the Specter*

"With darkly poetic prose and chilling stories that peel back layers of skin to reveal a beating, bloody heart, Eric LaRocca is the clear literary heir of Clive Barker." ~ Tyler Jones, author of *Criterium* and *The Dark Side of the Room*

WE
CAN
NEVER
LEAVE
THIS
PLACE

ERIC
LaROCCA

ISBN: 978-1-68510-023-0 (sc)
ISBN: 978-1-68510-024-7 (ebook)
Library of Congress Control Number: 2022931807

First printing edition: June 24, 2022
Published by Trepidatio Publishing in the United States of America.
Cover Artwork by Ble | Interior Papers: vector_corp freepik.jpg
Editing by Sean Leonard
Proofreading / Cover & Interior Layout: Scarlett R. Algee

Trepidatio Publishing, an imprint of JournalStone Publishing
3205 Sassafras Trail
Carbondale, Illinois 62901

Trepidatio books may be ordered through booksellers or by contacting:
JournalStone | www.journalstone.com

TREPIDATIO
PUBLISHING

This book belongs to you, dear heart.

WE

CAN

NEVER

LEAVE

THIS

PLACE

CHAPTER ONE

THERE ARE TIMES when I look back on moments from my life as if my recollections were living things, little organisms confined to glass vases I'm meant to nurture and care for. I regard them with the same fondness of a gardener as he observes a small bud sprouting from a freshly potted plant, a collector of living things that would perish without his gentle care.

Just like chrysanthemums planted in dry soil, or a neglected cactus, I often wonder if my memories would shrivel and crisp until black like delicate wreaths of ivy abandoned in daylight. I wonder if after a prolonged absence they might wither and close like poppies at sunset.

There are some recollections of mine with sprawling roots so strong I can't help but wonder if they're made from piano wire. Even if they were memories I might not care to attend to, like perennials they bloom every year around the same time, as if to remind me of the young woman I once was and how everything was almost taken from me.

It was, in fact.

From baby teeth to virginity, to live is to regularly suffer loss.

However, I scarcely expected to lose everything I've ever loved in a single moment.

The memory screeches at me like a newborn, a reminder that usually teases my mind when the television has been cranked up loud or when I notice a small spider circling a bowl of sugar in the kitchen. Little things that take me back to a certain time and place—the life from which I had once run away.

I can't help but recall how the air hung heavy like a damp curtain over our little apartment in one of the last remaining tenement buildings in the city, the air pulsing with electricity the same way it does before a summer storm—a gentle warning that something terrible was about to happen.

It came in the shape of a large man wearing a gas mask standing at our door. I can still recall the coppery scent of blood and sweat clinging to him as he stirred there. He resembled something like a primordial insect—something vile and monstrous that crawled from the sludge when the earth was forming and new. His eyes scanned me behind blood-rinsed goggles, his breath growling softly like the engines of the military planes that circled our city day and night.

"Can we come in?" he asked me, pushing his face against the small door slot I had opened as if threatening to enter with or without invitation.

I swallowed, clutching the small doll I always carried with me, made from embroidered cloth—the very same one my father had brought back for me after one of his trips to America. I clung to the doll as if I were clutching the few remaining threads of hope that we would ever venture there—a place where we wouldn't have to live in constant fear, a place where we could be free.

The man in the gas mask stirred again, impatient. "Can we come in or not?"

I sensed my body tensing as if my very skeleton had crystalized.

"No," I said, guarding myself with the word.

The man in the gas mask huffed, tugging on something I could not see. It was then I noticed another dark figure stirring beside him—a shorter man wearing a black tagelmust and eyes secreted behind dark goggles. What little was shown of the man's face was gaunt, as sunken cheekbones framed an easily frowning mouth. His eyes were wide and cautious like a nocturnal predator stalking defenseless prey.

"That must be his daughter," the man in the tagelmust whispered, his voice pinched and delicate sounding as if delighted they had finally found me.

The man in the gas mask narrowed his eyes at me with dangerous intent.

"Open the door," he said, knocking his fist against it.

"Not while my father's away," I said, fumbling for the latch and threatening to close the small window.

Just then, the man in the gas mask shoved his gloved fingers through the slot. "We have him with us," he said.

I didn't believe him.

Besides, my father had always taught my mother and me to never open the door unless he was home. "Derelicts and vagrants will use any excuse to get inside," he had once warned me. "I'm counting on you to keep your mother safe while I'm away." After all, the remnants of our home were one of the few things we had left. I would have sooner died than see what was left of our home become desecrated by two faceless castaways.

I glared at the man in the gas mask, my eyes shouting at him, "You're lying."

He recoiled slightly as if understanding my wordless message, removing his fingers from the door slot. "See for yourself," he said.

Cautious, I peered out from the small window and noticed something lying on the floor beside their feet—the outline of a body draped with blood-spattered linen. It was then I made a horrible recognition—a lifeless arm sprawling from beneath the sheet and showcasing my father's gold wristwatch.

I shook my head in disbelief.

It couldn't be true.

I pried open the door a mere sliver, my eyes following the man in the gas mask as he lowered to the body arranged at our doorstep. He knelt, lifting the sheet slightly, and it was then I recognized the truth—my father, his eyes closed, and his arms stretched at both sides as if he were a portrait of a holy man welcoming home a penitent sinner. I sensed the color drain from my face as I stared at the body, my eyes unblinking.

"Is your mother home?" the man in the gas mask asked, his voice thinning to a whisper.

The man in the tagelmust inched closer toward me and, for once, I did not shrink away. It was as if I couldn't move—I was nothing more than an infant sparrow who had fallen from its nest and broken its wing.

"A sniper," he explained. "Waiting on the roof."

My breath whistled, mouth hanging open in disbelief as the man in the gas mask tossed the sheet to cover my father's face.

"We checked his pockets. Found his papers. We wanted to…return him."

I winced slightly, the words "return him" like a small dagger twisting in my gut. I did my best to compose myself, drawing in a breath and then exhaling.

"Please come in," I said, opening the door further.

Just then, the embroidered doll slipped from my hands and crumpled beside my father's dead body the same way a dog might retreat to its dying owner. With it, I abandoned all hope my father had ever instilled in me.

Things would be different now.

Once they had dragged the body inside, I closed the door behind them as if I were shutting the massive entryway to a deserted tomb—a place I knew I would never leave, a place that would eventually digest me slowly like a large carnivorous plant.

There was nothing I could do but wait.

CHAPTER TWO

"**M**ARA. COME HELP me," my mother called to me from the nursery as she soaked my father's ash-caked body with a damp washcloth.

However, I was far too busy, preoccupied with doodling in the small antique leather-bound journal my father had once gifted me when he had returned from a trip to Cairo. I marveled at the small creature I had drawn in the margins of the empty page—a unicorn with its horn severed.

Just then, my ears perked at the sounds of shouting outside. I rose from the corner of the room, passing by the giant arm of a broken sewage pipe dangling and leaking there. I drifted across the floor—a dark mirror with an inch of sewage.

I arrived in the nursery.

"It's about time," my mother said, milling about the room with a rag and a rust-eaten bucket of cold water. "Scrub his feet, won't you?" she asked, pushing the rag across the mattress toward me.

But I didn't hear her.

Instead, I was drawn to the noises of shouting outside in the streets.

I approached the window sealed with plywood, slivers of sunlight flickering at me. Peering through one of the cracks, I sensed my face whitening as my eyes drifted down to the street below. It was there I saw a small boy—no older than thirteen or fourteen—scampering down the tenement-flanked dirt lane, ash circling in the air as distant fires blinked in the shattered windows of the other buildings. I looked closely: his eyebrows were popping with beads of sweat as he scurried along like a helpless insect avoiding daylight at all costs. His eyes were wide and fearful, as if he knew full well he were nothing more than prey being hunted.

Just as I was about to call out to him, a hailstorm of bullets hammered him to his knees. They travelled at him from every direction, as if a barrage of carefully trained ammunition had been stalking him. His little body exploded, ripped apart by giant invisible hands before he finally dropped to the ground, lifeless and steaming with wisps of smoke.

"Mara, away from the window," my mother said.

I covered my mouth, pulling myself away from the plywood-covered window, sewage lapping at my bare feet as I drifted to my mother.

I watched as she adjusted the violet-colored head scarf she had wrapped around her head as if embarrassed of her naturally greying hair, as if it were wicked for a woman to age not so gracefully. I noticed she quivered slightly—a private moment of visible defeat as she clutched her swollen stomach.

It was eight months yesterday.

I watched as she cleared the dampness from her eyes. Then she passed me a washcloth.

"Help me finish cleaning him," she said, soaking her husband's lifeless chest with a cloth and cleaning out the leaking exit wounds in his stomach and shoulder. "We'll dress him after."

"Dress him?"

Before my mother could answer, my small red canary named Kali sailed into the room and perched above the nursery's mirror, already dripping white with excrement like fresh paint. My mother rolled her eyes at the sight of the poor little creature—another reminder of my father's love for me. She merely squeezed the towel over the half-filled bucket and resumed her labor.

"For our guests," she said.

"We're expecting?"

I didn't want anyone else in our home. I certainly didn't expect them. I merely wanted to be left alone.

"It's the way it works," my mother explained, scrubbing my father's body violently as if she were attempting to remove the bullet holes in his chest, but those were things she would never be able to undo.

I sensed my grip loosening about the towel and it slipped from my hands, landing in the sewage at my feet. I closed my eyes, trembling. When I opened them, I noticed my mother staring at me—not with a look of judgment, but rather with a desperation I had never encountered before.

"Mara," she said, tossing the rag into the bucket. "I need you to promise me something. You won't say..."

Her words trailed off for an instant, as if her voice were breaking apart. Quickly, she recovered a firm plea.

"I don't want them knowing that he left us," she said, her face flushing with embarrassment.

My face scrunched, puzzled. I could scarcely believe what my mother was saying.

"Is that what you think?"

My mother reached across the bed, gently touching my hand. Her pruned skin was as transparent as wax paper. "Promise me you won't tell them," she begged.

I looked to my father's body, as if somehow believing he'd lift his head and dismiss her as he often did.

"But it's not true," I said.

"Mara—"

My mother pulled at me, but I shimmied away.

"He would never leave us," I said. "I know he wouldn't. He only left to barter for more food."

My mother's eyes spiraled at the notion. "And took his bags with him—"

"—to go to the market," I said, cutting her off.

My mother folded her arms, shaking her head. "It's been flooded for weeks."

"He said the allies would come to save us any day," I told her. "We have to wait."

My mother recoiled like a cottonmouth from unexpectedly more hostile prey. She lowered her head, lips moving with muted words at first. Finally, she opened her mouth to speak.

"He left us," she said, her voice brittle-thin like a dying insect.

The thought arrived in my mind as soon as she uttered the words—the horrible recollection I had sponged from my brain of my father packing his valise earlier today, dressing himself in his Sunday best, and whispering to me, "Be good while I'm away," as he stood at the doorway. I had scarcely imagined he had meant it would be for good.

"He promised he never would," I said, tears webbing in the corners of my eyes. I flicked them away with my index fingers.

My mother whimpered quietly, as if hurt by the secret world I and her husband had once shared.

"I don't know what he promised you," she said, straining to clear the catch in her throat. "I don't want them knowing he was killed after abandoning his family."

I couldn't help but wonder if she was perhaps right. Yes, it was possible. After all, there's a language shared between adults that children don't seem to understand—a secret language where intentions are clearer, and motivations are far more obvious. There were things passed between my parents I was told I would never understand, as if they were secrets from ancient civilizations of how to undo the universe.

"It's not true," I said, as if I were trying to convince myself. "He didn't leave us."

My mother looked away, rising from where she was kneeling and swiping away the bucket. "When you're finished cleaning him, his other suit's hanging in the closet," she said.

As she drifted out of the room, the small canary chirped at her.

"And put that thing back in its cage!" she yelled, disappearing underneath the white sheet hanging in the nursery's doorway.

It felt so peculiar to be left alone with him, as if I were in the presence of some strange, sleeping deity. The trouble was that no matter how much I yelled or cried, I knew he would never wake.

As I leaned over the mattress to smear the washcloth along his thigh, I noticed something crawling along my father's shoulder—a small spider. A skittering black-velvet body with eight pipe-cleaner legs. The creature scurried across my father's white linen-covered face.

As I swatted the creature away, my careless fingers dragged the cloth down and revealed my father's hideous death mask—his eyes closed and mouth open, as if in a permanent state of awe. Even in death, his defining imperfection remained: a reddish birthmark leeching across the side of his face like a dark shadow.

Realizing I was staring, I tossed the cloth over him until he was fully covered once more.

Out of the corner of my eye, I couldn't help but notice the spider scurry off, disappearing inside a small hole in the wall.

The tiniest, softest part of me took comfort in knowing that this was his home too.

CHAPTER THREE

IT WAS LATER that same afternoon when one of my mother's friends, Naomi, visited the apartment. She was a tall woman with auburn hair trimmed short in a pixie cut. As was her custom, she never arrived empty-handed.

"I came as soon as I heard," she said, passing a small plate of food wrapped in tin foil to my mother.

They wrapped their arms around one another, my mother's face disappearing in Naomi's shoulder for a moment as she sobbed gently.

"I'm so sorry," Naomi said, rubbing my mother's back.

After a few moments, they separated, and Naomi dabbed my mother's eyes.

"How did he—?" Naomi could scarcely bring herself to say the vile word.

My mother paled, as if she had been quietly dreading the question ever since Naomi had arrived.

I watched her, crouching from behind the safety of a wooden plank boarded up over the exposed paneling.

My mother locked the apartment door, visibly rehearsing her answer.

"He…went to barter for more food," she said, as if the idea had abruptly sprung into her mind.

Naomi's face scrunched, eyes searching my mother for an explanation.

"Alone?" she asked, studying her.

I watched as my mother turned away from Naomi, secreting the lie written across her face.

"He insisted."

Naomi swiped my mother's hands, rubbing them together. "What can I do?"

I watched my mother pull away, leading Naomi from the entryway into the living room piled with crates and boxes filled with junk. My mother snatched the remote control from the sofa, aimed it at the television flickering with bands of static, and shut it off.

"You do enough," she told Naomi. "We're fine."

Naomi tugged on my mother's sleeve, doggedly pursuing her around the room as my mother began to clear places on the moth-eaten couch for them to sit.

"Don't be stubborn," Naomi said.

"You treat me like a child," my mother exhaled, clearing dirty dishes aside.

"More food?" Naomi asked, taking a seat on the couch. "We don't have much, but you're welcome to it."

My mother stammered slightly, embarrassed.

"If...you think you have enough to share," my mother said, her eyes avoiding Naomi at all costs.

"Done. What else?"

"Nothing. I promise," my mother assured Naomi, sitting beside her.

"We can have the body removed after the service."

My mother's head swiveled at Naomi, disgust wrinkling her face. "And put where?" she asked. "A grave with thirty others? I promised I'd never do that to him."

Naomi began looking around the room, her eyes drifting from the bedsheets hanging in the open doorways and billowing like specters to the giant crack splitting the ceiling in half.

"Where's Mara?" she asked, searching the room for me.

I ducked behind the plywood covering the small opening in the wall until I was sure I was fully hidden.

"Hiding somewhere," my mother said, her eyes rolling. "Writing or drawing, probably. I hated how he always encouraged it."

Naomi simpered, smiling. "She's a storyteller."

"Just another word for 'liar,'" my mother said, folding her arms.

"She's okay?" Naomi asked, her voice clearly trembling with concern.

Thank God somebody still cares about me, I thought to myself.

"She helped me dress him," my mother explained. "She'll be fine. You worry about her too much."

"You don't worry enough."

My mother flinched slightly, as if surprised by Naomi's brashness. Her mouth wrinkled. But there was nothing to say.

"Something like this...can turn a young girl into a woman," Naomi said.

My mother's eyes merely flashed a threat. "Let's hope so," she said.

"For all the wrong reasons," Naomi explained. "She needs someone to care for her."

My mother responded in the only way she knew how—lowering her head, eyes mournful. "Who's going to care for me?"

Just then, a sliver of light glimmered across my face as I crouched behind the plywood.

My mother's gaze snapped to me with a wordless threat.

Shrinking, I slid the wooden board over the small opening and scurried away as if I were nothing more than a mere insect.

In her eyes, I probably was.

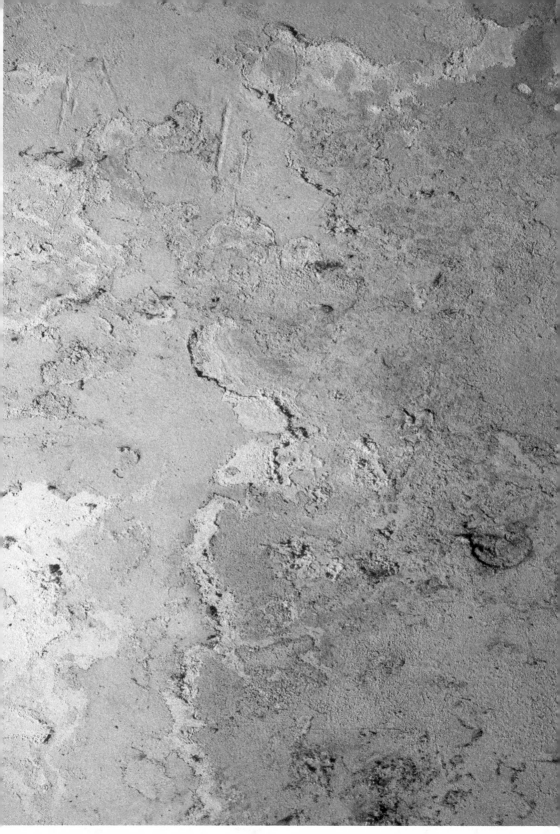

CHAPTER FOUR

AS I DRIFTED into the nursery filled with somber-faced guests dressed in expensive-looking black, I couldn't help but feel like a small island surrounded by dark water blooming with poison. I scratched my arm—a nervous habit I had yet to break—as my gaze darted around the room from guest to guest, straining to recognize a familiar face. Watching as the crowd of mourners filed beside my father's neatly dressed corpse to pay their final respects, I lowered my eyes until I arrived at the floor and saw my reflection staring back at me in the water.

I couldn't help but notice how there were new lines growing about my mouth and wrinkles set in the corners of my eyes, as if I had somehow been touched by something that had robbed me of my youth. I knew exactly what it was—death.

Clutching my embroidered doll, still stained with some of my father's blood, I watched my mother as she stood in the next room, guests surrounding her and offering their hands as their lips moved with muted condolences.

Without warning, my feet pulled me from the corner of the room and further into the crowd of strangers. Searching every face, I couldn't help but listen to their conversations as I passed through.

"You think they're still coming?" one of the guests asked another.

"If they don't make it, we'll have to wait for the ones coming from the north," another explained.

"That could take months," a mourner said. "We won't wait. Half of the block's already left."

I skirted around another small group of guests, leaning closer as they gossiped.

"—she was so much older," a woman dressed in black said. "We never understood it. He was practically a child."

One of the guests glanced at me out of the corner of his eye. "She's old enough to be the girl's grandmother."

I lowered my head, hurrying past them until I arrived on the outskirts of another small coterie arranged near the nursery's doorway.

"What else did they find?" a man asked.

"They had eaten the baby's eyes," the other guest replied.

My attention snapped to them, face paling.

"The poor mother."

"They killed her too," the guest said. "Raped her. Then, tore her limb from limb."

Just then, I slammed into my mother.

She said nothing to me, but rather regarded me as though I were an unwelcome visitor—a painful reminder of the life she had never wanted. Cowering away, embarrassed, I skulked as my mother turned to address the crowd of onlookers.

Clearly not used to speaking in front of large crowds, my mother's eyes avoided her guests as her voice thinned to a mere whisper when she spoke.

"I wanted to thank you all…for coming today," she said. "To remember…the great man my husband was. He wasn't the love of my life. He was…my savior. He saved me from a darkness that I couldn't get rid of. Not until he came. I know he would've been touched by your kind words and how generous you've been to me and my daughter."

She rubbed her stomach gently, sniveling.

"And our new one on the way," she said.

Naomi appeared at my mother's side, wrapping an arm around her.

"When we lost…our first child," my mother said, choking on quiet sobs, "…he would've been twenty this week. When we lost him. I was reminded…that everything that happens to you…is a gift. Even…sadness. Our daughter. Mara. She…was that gift."

The crowd stirred like a school of fish shifting with the tide. All eyes were glued to me as I backed into a corner, my cheeks heating red.

"Mara will be turning sixteen in three days," my mother explained, approaching me with mournful eyes.

"I'm sorry, sweet girl," she told me. "But I can hope you'll learn that the greatest sacrifices are met with the greatest gifts. Even something as horrible as this. I promise."

I wasn't comforted in the least, however, and I was certain she could tell.

My mother turned, addressing the crowd once more. "Mara is—"

She bit her lip, as if stopping herself from saying the word "liar."

"—a storyteller," she continued, resuming her speech. "Always encouraged by her father. I thought it would be special if she told us a story that she remembers of him."

My mother eyed me, silently commanding me from the corner where I was attempting to hide. I slowly inched out from my hiding spot with all the cautiousness of a fawn separated from its mother, my fingers tightening about the embroidered doll.

As soon as I approached her, my mother snatched the doll from my hands and tossed it aside. She eyed her guests, laughing to hide her visible nerves.

My breathing shallow, I turned to address the small crowd.

"My father…always," I began, the words splintering apart as they left my mouth. "He once said…"

I stammered, my breathing beginning to slow until it was ragged. Finally, panic set in as my gaze arrived at my mother—her glare of disappointment.

"I'm sorry," I said.

I elbowed my way through the crowd of bewildered guests, a voice whispering hideously in my ear: "Your mother was right. You are a liar."

CHAPTER FIVE

THE GUESTS DIDN'T stay long, and left shortly after I had abandoned the reception. I made myself busy by snatching Kali from her favorite perch above the bathroom mirror and relocating her to the small metal cage hanging from the ceiling in my bedroom.

Singing to her, I gently passed bits of food through the metal bars.

Out of my peripheral vision, I noticed my mother lift the white sheet covering the open doorway as she slid into the room. She knocked on the wall gently.

"Busy?" she asked.

I didn't look at her. I merely lowered my head, my hair hiding some of my face as I passed more little bits of food between the metal bars for Kali.

My mother hesitated, her eyes seeming as though they might hint at a peace offering.

"Thank you for putting her back in her cage," she said.

I began to rub my fingers along the length of the small cage. "She's not as happy when she's in there," I said.

Kali and I had that in common—in our separate cages.

My mother's face softened. "Come say goodnight to your father with me?" she asked, gesturing for me to follow her.

Without even waiting for me to react, she glided out beneath the sheet and disappeared down the hallway into the nursery. My feet pulled me after her, and it was only a few seconds before I was standing at the nursery's threshold, staring at the unmoving body of my father as he laid on the undressed mattress.

My mother lit a small candle and passed it to me. Then she lit another and arranged it in a small holder on the nightstand beside the bed.

I watched as my mother knelt beside my father, her hand touching his.

"Goodnight, my love," she said. "Sweet dreams."

Then she leaned against him and pressed her lips against his lifeless mouth. I winced, watching as she pushed harder against him—as if her very touch would revitalize him and bring him back to life somehow.

My mother turned gently, smirking as if amused by my uneasiness.

"Don't be scared," she said, extending her arm as if in an invitation to draw me closer.

For some reason, I obeyed, and I was at her side in a matter of seconds.

Hiding my discomfort as much as I could, my eyes wandered to my father's mouth—wrinkled and chapped like an untreated scar.

"You can kiss him, you know," my mother said, ushering me closer to him.

Yes, of course I knew that. But did I want to?

Sensing my mother's eyes lingering on me, I pursed my lips and gently pecked my father on his nose.

My mother smiled, for once proud of something I had done.

"See. There's nothing to be afraid of," she said. "It's still him. He's still with us."

But I could tell my face said otherwise, my stomach already doing somersaults at the mere notion of my father remaining with us.

As I lifted myself from my knees, the candle tilted in my hand, and wax dribbled on my father's collar.

"Careful," my mother said.

She snatched a nearby washcloth and dabbed my father's shirt until it was clean.

"He'll have to leave soon. Won't he?" I asked.

My mother recoiled at the question, her mouth crumpling. "Leave?"

"To be buried."

I could tell the word visibly scared her for a moment—*buried*. I watched as she searched herself for an answer. Recovering, she approached me with the preparedness of a skilled artisan.

"Don't you wish he could stay here with us?" she asked.

"But, he's—"

"You love your father. Don't you?" she asked, cutting me off.

I nodded.

"Then say goodnight to him."

As she had instructed, I knelt beside my father's bed and kissed his hand—his skin cold against my lips.

"I love you," I said to him.

Satisfied with my obedience, my mother steered me out of the nursery and back down the corridor toward my bedroom.

I climbed into bed, swiping my notebook and pencil from the nightstand, and began to write. I glanced up, noticing my mother loitering in the doorway.

"Goodnight, Mara," she said.

I lowered my pencil. Then, forced a polite smile. "Goodnight."

My mother shifted in the doorway, about to leave, when suddenly she turned and inched closer toward my bed.

"I just want to say—I'm sorry," she said. "For forcing you to say something in front of all those people. I did it because…"

Her voice trailed off, as if searching for the right word. I decided to help her.

"Because Naomi always calls me a 'storyteller,'" I said.

My mother sat on the edge of the bed, folding her hands and furrowing her lips, her face a mask of guilt.

"No," she said. "I did it…because I wanted to hurt you. Because I thought making you feel worse about it…would make me feel better. I'm sorry."

Of course, that's what I had thought. But I had never expected her to admit to the fact. I lifted myself out of bed, pushing my paper and pencil aside. There was something I had always wanted to tell her—something that had lingered between us in private spaces since I was very little as if it were a ghost: a spirit that fed on our willingness to ignore it.

"Father once told me a story called, 'Lament for a Lost Unicorn,'" I told her. "And…it was about a beautiful unicorn a blind man and his wife found. One night, someone broke into the stable and tried to steal it. Even though he was able to rescue it, he knew others would come and do worse. So he took a hacksaw and cut off its horn until it resembled a horse."

It was then I noticed my mother's eyes were shimmering wet. She knew the story too.

"'Why?' the poor creature asked him," my mother said, picking up the narration.

"Yes," I said, smiling. "'How could you do this to me?' the creature asked. And the blind man said, 'I wanted to be the only one to hurt you.'"

My mother looked off, distant and dreaming. "I remember that story. My mother told it to me," she said.

"He told me it for the first time in the car ride back from the circus," I explained.

"Which time?" my mother joked. "You went so much we thought you'd join."

"He always cried when he told me that story," I said, my speech slowing as I recalled my father—his head lowered as if in prayer—as he had finished reciting the story to me.

It was then I made the horrible realization—perhaps my mother was right. He did leave us.

"I think you're right," I told her.

My mother tilted her head at me, confused. "About what?"

I couldn't bear to say the words. I merely flashed my mother a solemn look, and she seemed to understand in the way that most mothers and daughters are able to secretly communicate. She wrapped her arms around me, swaddling me until I was choked.

"He loved you," she said, pecking my forehead with a kiss. "Still does."

My mother heaved herself off my bed and began to amble toward the doorway when something pulled her back—an invisible hand drawing her back to my bedside.

"Mara," she said, "there's something I need from you. I've kept a lot from you. Too much. I regret that. Especially about your brother and how he—"

I couldn't stop the words. They came hurtling from deep inside the pit of my throat:

"Father told me you said it was my fault," I said.

I recoiled, as if surprised I had even said it.

My mother's eyes lowered, embarrassed.

"Yes. I didn't mean it," she said, wincing as if the words hurt her to say. "This whole time. We could've been…so much closer. But maybe this will change things. Losing someone you love. It always changes everything. So, maybe it'll change us?"

I sensed myself softening, as if enchanted by the idea. Yes, perhaps it was somehow possible—out of something so horrible can come something so good.

"I'd like that," I said, pulling the bedsheets over me until I was swallowed.

Then, my attention drifted to my notebook beside me. A little reminder—a peace offering.

I opened the journal and ripped out a handful of pages.

"I've started writing a new story," I said. "About Father and everything that has happened."

My hands trembling, I gently held out the papers for my mother to take as if I were approaching a wild dog—something that could turn and snip at me in an instant.

"It's not finished," I explained. "But I want you to read it."

My mother pulled the sheets of paper from my hands, coveting them. Her face flushed with warmth.

"Thank you," she said. "What do you call it?"

"'Lament for a Lost Girl.'"

My mother smiled, clearly amused. "I like that."

She turned, about to leave once more, when she swiveled back to me with another look of pleading. "Mara. I need you to promise me you'll accept these changes," she said. "Whatever they may be. Just know they're for the best."

I considered for a moment, noticing her eyes glued on me.

"Yes," I said. "I promise."

My mother smiled, gently touching my hand the same way I had apprehensively touched my father's body—careful not to upset me, as if I were marked "Fragile, handle with care."

As I looked down at her hand, I noticed something—a white thread wrapped around my mother's index finger on her right hand. Tied so tight it appeared to be cutting off circulation. The skin around the fingernail—swollen purple with blood.

I stared until my mother pulled her hand away from me. She was smiling, as if pleased I had noticed.

CHAPTER SIX

IT WAS NOT long after midnight when my eyelids started to feel heavy.

My mind continued to wander, sleep a distant thought. As soon as I rolled over onto my side, I sensed something warm and wet collecting between where my legs met.

Not again, I thought to myself.

Slipping my hands beneath the sheets, I slid off my underwear and balled them into a fist. My hand was sticky with blood.

Shifting out of bed, I tiptoed across the room and over to a small hole in the wall. Wincing, as if I were burying a part of myself—a part of my womanhood—I pushed the blood-soaked underwear deep inside the small opening until it finally disappeared from sight.

I looked around the dark room, as if fearful someone somehow might have played witness to my shame—my unwanted monthly reminder of being a young woman. My eyes drifted to Kali as she sat perched on the small handlebar in her iron cage. I went over to her, opening the small door to pet her, when she launched herself out and sailed out of the room.

I followed the little bird into the hallway, where she eventually disappeared, and it was then I heard the sounds of my mother sobbing in her bedroom—long, deep, guttural groans like the sound of a speared animal. I noticed a sliver of candlelight from my mother's room bleeding into the narrow corridor, the sounds of her agony filling the apartment. I turned, bewildered, and immediately noticed a dark yellow glow flickering at the foot of the nursery door.

Tiptoeing down the hallway, I lifted the sheet and skirted into the nursery, where I found my father's body—dressed in his suit as he was before—surrounded by a bright halo of melting candles. Light shimmered across the floor's watery screen as I inched into the room.

My ears perked at the noise of something stirring behind me.

I turned and found my mother standing at the doorway with a fistful of papers—my story. Her lips curled with fury, her eyes smoldering with a dangerous threat.

"How could you?" she asked, her voice trembling.

My mind raced, wondering what she could possibly mean. It wasn't as if the story I had given her presented her in an unfavorable light. I wrote the truth, though I suppose the truth for a fifteen-year-old is vastly different than the truth of a grown woman. Regardless, I already had an apology rehearsed.

"I didn't—" I began to say.

"This…is what you think of me?" my mother asked, brandishing the crumpled sheets of paper. Her tongue flicked out so violently that I wondered if it forked in the middle. "This is how you see your mother?"

"I didn't mean to—"

My mother answered before I could finish, crushing the papers in her hand.

"Your father left because of you," she told me. "Did you know that? He hated what you reminded him of."

I sensed myself weakening, my knees quivering as if I were a single word away from being blown over like a rootless plant.

"That's not true," I said, my voice a mere whisper.

"He was embarrassed," she said. "So he left. He died because he was trying to get away from you."

I wiped away the tears already beading in my eyelashes. I wouldn't give her the satisfaction of seeing me cry. Not again.

"Nothing's ever going to change what you and I are to each other," my mother said, tossing the crumpled sheets of paper at me before storming out of the room and disappearing down the corridor.

As I knelt down to collect the paper floating at my feet, I heard a knock at the main door.

It was a gentle knock—polite, gracious. Not the thunderous clanging we typically heard when the different militias would make rounds in the neighborhood to document everybody's papers.

I rubbed my eyes, my vision blurring, as I approached the door. My eyes wandered to a small moth fluttering beside the door in the apartment entryway. The tiny insect glued itself to the wall, wings tucked and closing like curtains, as if it were waiting for something.

As I slid the lock out of the slot and opened the small window fixed at the center of the doorway, I was greeted by an empty hallway. The dim corridor stretched on a slant like a carnival slide for fifty yards. The end of the hallway—a gaping maw of exposed brick and metal overlooking the street four stories below.

I squinted, blinking, as my eyes struggled to focus on a shape shifting in the darkness where the corners of two collapsed structures met. Just then, a bird—a whisper of wings and a vivid flash of black—flitted down the hall and roosted in a small nest arranged above the doorway to an abandoned apartment.

Frowning, I closed the window and fastened the lock.

As I moved away from the door, another knock came. Louder, as if insisting.

My fingers fumbled with the latch and I slid the small window open again. This time, I was greeted by a domed head with wool-like hair as dark as charcoal, filling most of the window frame. Eight massive eyes—black as onyx and glistening—investigated my every movement. The creature loosened small fleece-jacketed claws set beside his face and began to clean his mouth.

"May I come in?" he asked, voice brittle thin.

I found myself recoiling, gazing at my reflection in his enormous mirror-like eyes.

"Who are you?" I asked.

"I expect your mother will want to see me," he said, pushing one of his hair-covered legs through the window as if impatient. "Would you tell her I'm here?"

He flexed his mouth, revealing a glistening pair of needle-thin fangs.

Without hesitation, I slammed the window shut and locked the latch. As I retreated from the door, I stumbled into my mother. She stood there in her nightgown, scowling at me.

"Who was it?" she asked.

I trembled, out of breath.

"There's something…" I began to say, my voice trailing off as if unsure. "They say…they're here to see you."

"And you slam the door in their face?" she asked, shoving past me and threatening to undo the latch.

Just as she slid the lock open, I grabbed the bolt from her and fastened it shut again.

"No. Don't," I begged her.

But before I could persuade her, she shoved me away.

"Out of the way," she said, unbolting the door.

As the door creaked open, light spilled out into the hallway and revealed the strange creature in all his monstrous glory. Eight massive fur-lined spindles fanned out in a velvet wreath as he clutched the frame of the doorway. The underside of his abdomen was formed in the shape of a human skull.

His suspended body—needle-thin bristles of fur woven with ribbons of emerald and silver—shifted as if tirelessly searching for a modicum of comfort when none was to be had. He carried with him the metallic scent of gunfire—a sulfurous stench pearling about his body as if it were a part of him. When he spoke, it sounded as if wet cement had been poured into his throat.

My mother shrank at the sight of the giant spider hanging in our doorway.

"Hello?" she said.

The creature relaxed his grip, legs crumpling as he lowered his body from the door frame.

"Dear heart. Please forgive the lateness," the spider said.

I watched my mother as she squinted at him, studying him as more of his massive body arrived in the light.

"Do I know you?" she asked.

"I was pained to hear of your loss," he said. "May I offer you my sincerest condolences?"

I noticed my mother began to relax, warmth heating her cheeks.

"That's very kind of you," she said. "Please. Come in."

I recoiled as I watched the giant spider crawl across the threshold and scamper into the apartment.

"You're a most gracious host," the creature said, eyeing me.

"What can we do for you?" my mother asked.

"It's not what you can do for me, dear heart," he said, stirring in place. "It's what I can do for you."

My mother glanced at me and then back at the spider. "What…can you do for us?"

Without warning, the creature scaled the wall, its pedipalps flexing with excitement as if pleased she had asked.

"I imagine you were abandoned with far more than the absence of mere affection," he said. "Perhaps a feeling of safety went wandering too."

I noticed my mother seemed to weaken at the reminder, her eyes lowering and shoulders dropping.

The giant spider crept up the honeycombed wall paneling until he twirled upside down, dangling from the ceiling by a mere thread of silk.

"I'll only be too glad to protect you, dear heart," he said, eyes scanning me and flickering with hunger. "The both of you. In exchange for a very modest compensation."

Of course he would expect something. Why wouldn't he? I stared at my mother, silently begging her to send him on his way. But she wouldn't even look at me.

"Yes?" she said.

"Food," the creature said. "Anything you'd be willing to spare."

I watched my mother smile, relieved, as if she had expected something far worse.

"We have more than enough," she said, gesturing for him to follow her to the kitchen.

I couldn't take it anymore. I wouldn't let my mother desecrate our home with some uninvited guest.

"No," I said.

My mother turned, glaring at me as if shocked I said something. "Mara. Please. He's—"

She stopped herself, face paling. "I'm sorry," she said to him. "I don't know your—"

"Rake," he said, bowing. "No need for formalities."

He scampered across the ceiling until he cornered me against the wall, extending one of his legs to me.

"Dearest Mara," he said. "I'm sorry to meet you under these circumstances."

But I wouldn't budge. I folded my arms, refusing his.

"Mara," my mother said. "Don't be rude to our guest."

Rake withdrew from me, simpering slightly. "She looks as if she recognizes me," he said. "Those starry eyes. Like so many of my young fans."

My mother's eyes lit up, as if enchanted by the word.

"Fans?"

"Of course," Rake replied. "The circus yields a small following of devoted enthusiasts."

"The circus," my mother exhaled, pulling on my sleeve. "Mara, your favorite."

Rake cornered me once again. My nostrils twitched at the scent of gunfire shadowing him.

"Were you ever a patron of the Shrine and Ladder Brothers Circus?" he asked me. "Pitiful accommodations. But. Marvelous attractions. My act was their most famous. I had lines of young women. Stretching for miles. Just to bring me things to eat."

I glared at him with a look of uncertainty. I wanted him gone, and I wanted him to know it. He seemed amused by my incredulousness, chortling.

"She has the well-practiced look of a skeptic," he said to my mother. "A portrait of doubt. *Questioner Afraid of Answer.* Acrylic on canvas."

"Will you show us?" my mother begged.

I watched quietly as Rake's eyes moved to the wall, where he noticed the small moth.

"It's always the same invitation," he said. "Every time. 'Oh, but you don't mean you'd really eat anything,' they say. As if they expect me to provide them with a fork to poke through my shit and find the proof. No. Where's the excitement in that?"

Rake snatched the tiny insect from the wall with his massive pair of pincers, his fangs parting as he stuffed the moth inside and swallowed it whole.

I recoiled, covering my mouth in disgust.

"Not as flavorful as a beetle," he chirped. "But thankfully not as slimy as an earthworm."

My mother applauded, gaze following Rake as if permanently bewitched by his showmanship.

"After all. Won't insects be eating us one day?" Rake said, descending from the wall and scurrying toward me with a warning. "They're going to be devouring your father soon."

I looked to my mother, horrified, but she seemed to ignore the comment.

"Don't mistake my daughter's difficulty to impress with glumness," she said. "It's teenage disrespect. That's all."

"She's a discerning critic. I savor the prospect of a challenge," he said. "But first. I'm famished."

"Of course," my mother said, ushering him from the entryway. "Would you come pay your respects first?"

Rake bowed, agreeing as he followed her into the nursery. She turned, glaring at me.

"Are you going to join us?" she asked me.

I merely shook my head, my feet glued where I stood.

My mother responded with a wordless look of disappointment. Then she curled her fingers about one of Rake's legs. Once again, I noticed the white thread nearly severing my mother's index finger.

They disappeared into the nursery, their shadows flickering along the walls.

I found myself alone, listening to the hypnotic drip of the broken sewage pipe as it hung in the room like the arm of a lifeless giant.

Suddenly, a small black snake slithered across my feet, hissing. I lurched back, startled, and watched the little creature slither across the floor and vanish into a tiny hole in the wall.

CHAPTER SEVEN

MORNING LIGHT TRICKLED in through the wooden planks securing my bedroom window. I stirred beneath the sheets, stretching and yawning. It felt as though my head had been bandaged with plastic wrap and shoved inside an oven to melt, as if I were some expensive Parisian delicacy. I could sense the pulse of my heartbeat between my ears as if the organ inside my head were a fluttering moth, impatient to crack the eggshell of my skull apart and flit off toward freedom.

Hoisting my legs over the edge of the bed, my feet landed in an inch of sewage covering my bedroom floor. I glanced down, noticing bits of excrement bobbing along the murky surface.

As I swung out of bed, I noticed my beloved leather-bound journal floating beside the wall. My precious stories. I grabbed at the journal and tossed the sewage-soaked bundle on the bed.

Tiptoeing toward the sheet covering my bedroom doorway, I heard a sound I hadn't heard in our home for quite some time—laughter. Even stranger, it was the sound of my mother's laugh.

I skirted out into the hallway and meandered down the corridor until I finally arrived in the kitchen. There, I was met with my mother standing at the kitchen counter as she sliced a small loaf of bread. Rake hung above the table, as if waiting to be fed.

My mother glanced at me for a moment. Then she resumed her slicing.

"We didn't think you'd ever wake up," she said, the seriousness of her tone hinting she had secretly hoped I wouldn't.

"Dreams so pleasant you couldn't bear to part with them?" Rake asked.

I ignored him. Instead, my feet answered as they sloshed in the sewage water pooling at the kitchen's entrance.

"My room's flooded," I said. "The whole place—"

"Yes. That broken pipe," my mother hummed, arranging the sliced bread on one of our finest plates. "I've been meaning to fix it—"

"Something I could do?" Rake asked.

"You do enough," my mother assured him, setting the plate on the table.

The giant spider bowed, shoveling all the food into his mouth with his set of claws.

"That's two days' worth of rations," I said, staring at the empty plate in disbelief.

"Mara," my mother said, shooing me away. "Don't be rude. It was stale anyway."

"But he's eating everything."

"Mara, that's enough."

It was then I noticed the spider staring at me, his eight eyes following me as I skirted around the table.

"Mara. Come join me," he said. "Let me show you a trick from my act. One of my most renowned deceptions. I was discouraged to find my adoring fans had become less than pleased to watch me consume their offerings. Donations dwindled, and seats went unfilled for weeks."

I watched him, hypnotized, as he flattened one of his legs against the table's surface as if preparing for some sort of labor.

"It was when I nearly died during a performance that I realized they preferred to instead witness my suffering. All people are like that. Eager consumers of someone else's pain. Whether they know it or not. Why deny them what they want?"

Without warning, he ripped off his leg, tossing it in the sewage as if it were nothing more than a bent tree branch.

I covered my mouth, nearly retching at the gruesome sight.

"Be without fear, dear heart," he said.

With the finesse of a magician, Rake tucked his remaining seven legs beneath his abdomen as he suspended in mid-air. He waited for a moment, as if delighting in the exquisiteness of my uncertainty.

With an exaggerated flourish, he unfurled his legs to reveal—eight of them. All intact.

He bent his dagger-like appendage, curling his leg at me.

"See," he said to me. "Good as new."

My mother applauded wildly like a giddy schoolgirl.

"Wonderful," she exclaimed.

I merely folded my arms.

"Spiders do that all the time," I said, hoping I might hit him where it hurts. If he even could be hurt, that is.

"Mara," my mother said, chiding me.

Rake's eyes never left me.

"Do they, dear heart?" he asked, unfurling his fangs with a promise to use them.

I shuddered for an instant, but quickly steeled my resolve. I met his challenge, tipping a chair out from the table and sitting beside him.

"There's nothing special about it," I said.

He looked surprised by my brazenness, a decidedly quizzical look making its home across his face.

"Mara. One more disrespectful comment and I'll give your breakfast to him," my mother said, delivering a plate of freshly sliced grapefruit to the table.

As my gaze followed my mother's hand, I couldn't help but notice her index finger. It had been shortened by at least an inch; the small nub wrapped with white bandage already rusted brown with dried blood.

"Your finger," I said, pointing.

My mother immediately pulled away, tucking her finger into her apron pocket. She bit her lower lip, as if dismayed she had forgotten about it.

"Yes—when I was cutting the bread this morning," she stammered. "I'm surprised I didn't wake you."

"Don't worry, dear heart," Rake said. "I took care of your mother."

He glared at me with a similar invitation.

Before I could say anything else, there was a knock at the door.

"Mara, go and see who that is, won't you?" my mother asked, returning to the counter and brandishing the knife for her next task—half-rotted pomegranates.

I lifted myself out of the chair and hastened to the front door, sliding open the small latch. Naomi's face filled the small window.

"Hi, love," she said.

I closed the window and unfastened the lock, the door swinging open. Naomi pushed inside, pinching my cheeks as she passed.

"Where's your mother?" she asked.

I didn't quite know what to say—or rather, what to call him.

"She's with our new—"

Just then, I noticed Naomi's face scrunch, soured. She frowned, lifting her soaked feet as sewage lapped against her ankles.

"Still?" Naomi asked, throwing a look of disgust at me.

I merely shrugged.

43

Naomi huffed, passing into the living room as I followed her.

"I have news," she told me. "Where is she?"

My mother appeared in the kitchen doorway.

"You're too late," my mother joked. "The food's gone."

"Where are your bags?" Naomi asked, her eyes scanning the cluttered room.

My mother forced a half-hearted chuckle. "I'm teasing," she said. "We still have some left. Come before it's gone."

"We're leaving," Naomi said, seizing my mother's attention.

My mother's head snapped back to her in a double take.

"Tonight," Naomi said. "How fast can you both pack?"

"Leaving?" I asked, my voice quivering.

"To where?" my mother asked.

"Far away," Naomi replied, scouring through crates and half-empty boxes before recovering a small suitcase. "Pack now," she said, shoving the suitcase into my arms.

I turned to leave, but my mother stopped me.

"You can't leave," my mother said. "You'll be killed."

"It's a small group," Naomi explained. "One of Jacob's friends is leading us. He says he'll keep us safe. It'll take a day and a half to get to the border. Come with us."

My mother shook her head, plugging her ears. "You're not listening to me. It's not safe."

I watched as Naomi's eyes combed my mother's face as if struggling to recognize her. Then she glanced at me.

"You can't stay here forever," she whispered.

My mother responded, merely rubbing her swollen stomach. "I'll slow you down."

"We'll wait," Naomi assured her.

My mother shook her head, eyes closing. "I'm having this baby here," she said.

"At least give the child a chance to live," Naomi blurted out.

Her face paled, as if immediately regretful. She inched away from my mother, head lowering in humiliation. My mother winced, as if visibly hurt.

"We can never leave this place," my mother told her. "It would hurt too much."

Naomi grabbed at my mother's hand, but flinched as soon as she noticed my mother's bandaged finger. My mother pulled away, her face reddening.

"Please. Come," Naomi begged her.

"Excuse me," my mother said. "I have company."

I watched as Naomi's gaze followed my mother into the kitchen and beyond the bedsheet draped over the open doorway.

"Who's in there with her?" she asked me.

"He came late last night," I explained. "She says he's going to stay with us."

Suddenly, I saw panic flood Naomi's face, her eyes widening. She had seen something.

"Mara," she said, her voice trembling. "Go and pack your things."

I hesitated slightly. "She doesn't think we should—"

Naomi grabbed my hands, squeezing them together. "Please. Say you'll come."

My eyes drifted to the kitchen doorway where I saw the silhouettes of my mother and Rake thrown against the transparent curtain as they sat at the kitchen table.

I watched as Rake's shadow leaned in close to my mother, his mouth against her throat as if he were the ghost of a dejected lover. I looked closer, observing as he wrapped several legs around my mother's shoulders and squeezed tight.

I knew I couldn't leave her. Not like this.

"I…can't," I said, shaking my head.

Naomi deflated for an instant. Then her eyes were on me again, as if hopeful. "What can I say to change your mind?"

I thought for a moment. I knew exactly what I would want.

"Say we can bring my father with us," I replied.

Naomi looked at me confused. "Mara, your father's dead," she said.

Yes, perhaps to others he was. But not to me.

"I can't leave him," I told her.

Naomi lowered her head. Then she began to inch toward the door. "If you change your mind, we leave after midnight," she said.

I opened the door for her, swallowing hard.

I watched as Naomi searched me for an answer I would never divulge. When she realized she would go wanting for a reaction, she dropped her shoulders with disappointment and skirted out into the hallway, where she eventually disappeared from view.

Without warning, Rake and my mother pushed past me.

My mother carried large wooden planks and a hammer my father had once used to kill a snake we had found in our bathtub drain.

She leaned a plank against the door and sifted through her pockets for a nail. When she finally found one, she presented it to Rake.

He merely frowned.

"That's much too short, dear heart," he said. "They'll break down the door."

My mother, cringing at her own forgetfulness, sifted through her open palm, filled with a small collection of various types of nails.

"What are you doing?" I asked as I approached them slowly.

My mother wouldn't even look at me. She was far too preoccupied holding out her open palm for Rake to inspect.

"Protecting ourselves," she barked at me.

Finally, she produced a longer nail. Rake nodded, visibly pleased.

I watched as my mother pressed the plank against the front door and slammed the hammer into the nail. Again, and again.

I winced slightly, as if she were pounding the nail directly into my bones.

I didn't remain there for long. I retreated to my room and found Kali squatting in her cage. I cupped the remaining bag of grain I had left and spooned some into the bottom of her cage as I watched her feed.

It was then I noticed Rake appearing in the doorway.

"Fortune has favored you on this side of the door, dear heart," he said. "Don't you know there are monsters out there?"

Of course I knew that. He was one of them.

I ignored him as he mounted the wall, threads of silk spooling as he climbed.

"I know what you want," he said.

I lowered my guard for a moment. Perhaps he somehow did know. If he could perform magic with such verve, it was possible he knew exactly what I wanted. I eyed him, as if it were a challenge.

"Your father," he said.

I flinched, the two words spearing me as if I were swine to be sold at auction.

"A love like that is irreplaceable," he said, scurrying across the ceiling. "A young woman needs that. Otherwise she'll become misshapen. Easy to break."

I bit my lip, turning away from him as he approached and dangled above me.

"I can bring him back," he whispered.

My eyes snapped to him.

He couldn't possibly, I thought to myself. *Could he?*

"I can make it as if he had never left," Rake said, spinning gently above me.

I didn't believe him. I folded my arms and looked away.

"It's a love and protection I know I'll never be able to provide you," he explained. "At least not while your mother occupies most of my attention."

Just then, he cupped my chin with one of his legs and lifted my eyes to meet his gaze.

"I can make it so that you'll never go wanting for the same love," he said. "Not while I'm here."

"How?" I asked, my voice hoarse with fear.

"You'll see," he said. "But it may not be what you want at first. Sometimes a gift isn't."

I didn't quite understand.

He's just trying to trick me, I thought to myself.

"I'll make it so," Rake said. "As long as I have your compliance."

He eyed me, as if expecting a response for his bargain—a hint, anything to know I would be agreeable.

I hesitated, unsure. But I would do almost anything if it meant seeing my father again.

"If you bring my father back, you'll have it," I told him.

Rake said nothing. He merely stirred in his web the way all spiders do when they've trapped their prey.

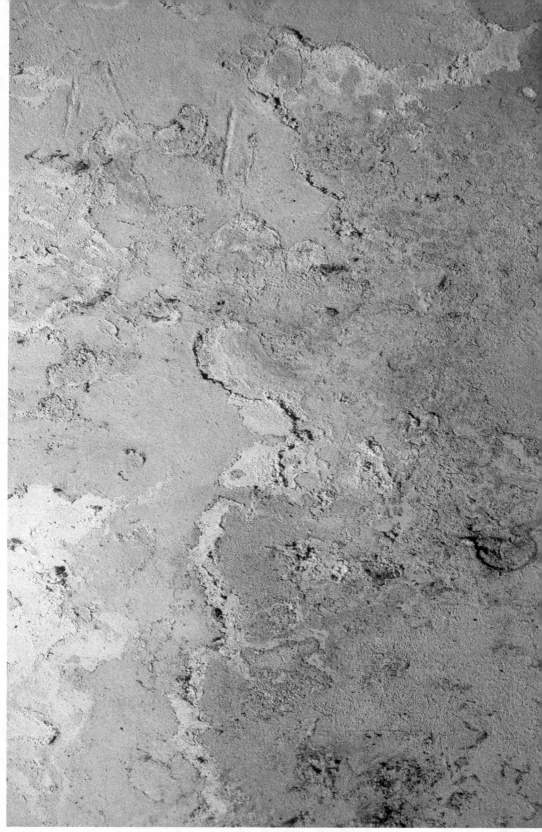

CHAPTER EIGHT

L ATER THAT NIGHT, my mother fetched me to help her reorganize the furniture in the living room until it resembled a small makeshift theater. Candles were arranged before the cartons and boxes comprising the performance space like oil-flame footlights.

What began as an invitation to perform one of his greatest tricks from his act became a three-hour spectacle showcasing his most revered illusions.

My mother watched with wonderment, wide-eyed like a bewitched child as Rake performed tirelessly for us.

I was instead more focused on the main doorway, boarded shut with wooden planks.

"Another request for my next exhibition?" Rake asked, skirting the rim of the giant cobweb he had used to blanket the living room wall.

"How about…the trick you showed us at lunch?" my mother asked.

Out of the corner of my eye I noticed Rake glaring at me, spying my disinterest. The giant spider grinned, approaching me.

"Sometimes I employed the practice of storytelling in my performances," he said. "In place of more…violent or disgusting theatrics."

His eyes narrowed at me.

"Your mother tells me you write stories, too?"

For some reason I looked to my mother as if in search of approval. There was none to be had.

"Sometimes," I whispered.

"There's not much excitement in talking about something horrible," he began, spinning a thread of silk from the ceiling as he hung there. "People want to see it. And why shouldn't they? I'd much prefer to show talent than let it float inside a toilet bowl. That's exactly what one young mother I had visited was planning to do. She called me Mr. Grace. And I referred to her as...Mrs. Melancholy. She had been a mother for eleven minutes. Until the blood-soaked bundle she had pushed out three months early turned purple and cold. In her despair she could've flushed it. Sent it to the sewers. To be pecked at by fish and rats. But instead. She kept it. Held on to it. Cared for it like it was still alive. Smashed food into its open mouth. Dressed it in clothes she had bought. A tiny red carrot in overalls two sizes too big. 'You can't help me,' she said. 'You can't get rid of my sadness.'"

Rake lowered himself in front of me, pressing his face against mine. "And there it was," he said. "The same test you gave me. So, I prepared the meal. And made her watch me eat. 'This is my gift to you,' I said. Its arms and legs. Rubbery like the limbs of a frog. Crunching like chicken bones. She was quiet even as she watched me suck out its eyes through my smile. And when I had finally cleaned the plate. I looked at her and said, 'I told you I'd make your sadness disappear.'"

I could sense my thin veneer of disinterest cracking like old paint, my stomach curling as he concluded his story. I spotted my mother's concern, as if she were ashamed of inviting him inside our home.

"And...Mrs. Melancholy?" my mother asked, her voice quivering as if fearful of the answer.

"She thanked me when it was finished," he explained. "As they all do."

Just then, there was the distant wail of a siren. The faint sounds of shouting outside the building.

"That sounds close," I said.

I watched as my mother shifted, uncomfortable.

"All this needless talking," she said. "It was supposed to be a pleasant evening." She eyed Rake, gesturing him to return to the makeshift stage. "Would you please do something else for us? A nice distraction."

Without warning, a bomb exploded outside.

The floorboards shook, the walls trembling as if they were made of rubber. We teetered like dolls in a capsized dollhouse.

After a few moments, the room settled with silence.

Then, another blast. This one—closer.

The whole apartment shuddered as the walls spiderwebbed with cracks. The floor split open, sewage water circling the hole as if it were a giant drain. As the ceiling buckled, debris swirled in the air and blanketed the room like a winter snow squall. I watched helplessly as Kali—a flash of crimson—fluttered about the room, frightened.

The ceiling finally separated, a giant hole opening and exposing the empty apartment on the floor above us. I watched Rake as he scaled the wall. For once, he seemed frightened—a pathetic insect.

The crack in the ceiling began to split further, and it was then I began to hear someone calling for help.

"There's somebody up there," I shouted to my mother.

But my cries were muted when another explosion rocked the building, the entire room shaking as the structure groaned like a sinking ship.

I covered my mouth as I watched the ceiling open, revealing a dark shape thrashing on the ledge—a giant black snake.

A flailing thread of shimmering scales dove off the ledge, crashing into the apartment. The creature's dirt-caked body coiled in a clump on the floor.

"Mara, come help me," my mother said, rushing to the creature's aid.

I reluctantly approached the unexpected guest. My eyes met his as he struggled to lift his head for a moment. The creature's jaw stretched, his amber-colored eyes dimmed and glassy.

My mother knelt beside him, shoving her hands beneath his body and struggling to lift him.

"I can't do it," she said. "Mara, help me."

Then there was a final explosion. The building trembled as bits of ceiling scattered in the apartment like debris sent from heaven.

I winced, lifting the creature's body and leaning him against a broken wooden post. I watched as my mother knelt beside the snake, inspecting him. She poked at his underside, revealing a glistening metal spike wedged in his abdomen. When she touched it, he thrashed. I sensed myself pouting—a stranger to my mother's tenderness.

"We have to help him," my mother told me.

My gaze darted to the creature when I found him staring at me, mouth parting. I noticed his tail slowing until it was finally without movement. My mother knelt, tucking her hand underneath the creature's body once more.

"Mara," she said, "help me carry him to your room."

I lurched back, startled by the order. "My room?"

"He needs our help," she insisted.

I folded my arms. "He can't stay here."

"Of course he can."

Rake scampered near me. "This could be a gift, dear heart," he whispered in my ear. "Remember what I told you."

"Anyone that needs our help is welcome here," my mother said. "Now, move him."

After we dragged the creature's body into my bedroom, my mother began to tend to his wounds as she bandaged his battered tail with fresh cloth. I knelt at her side with a bucket of water and a moth-eaten rag. Out of my peripheral vision, I saw Rake hanging from the doorway as he supervised.

I watched as my mother ran her fingers along the small bit of metal wedged in the snake's abdomen. He stirred, tail whipping back and forth.

"I'm sorry," she whispered to him.

She would never be so tender with me.

Without further hesitation, my mother wrenched the nail from the snake's underside. The poor creature writhed in agony.

"The dressings," she barked at me. "Quick."

As I passed the roll of dressings to my mother, our hands touched. It was then I noticed my mother's middle finger had been wrapped with silk thread. My mother didn't seem to notice my look of apprehension. She was far too concerned with her new houseguest, pressing the cloth against the creature's wound.

I watched as he flinched, eyes closing as his body relaxed.

"Keep pressure on this," my mother ordered.

"But—"

"Now," she growled.

I pressed my hand against the bandage as my mother lifted herself off her knees.

"He'll sleep in here tonight," she said.

"In here?"

But she didn't respond. She was already halfway out the door, following Rake.

"Where are you going?" I asked.

"Remember to hold down tight," my mother said as she left. "Until the bleeding stops."

I looked to Rake, searching for an explanation.

"Do as your mother says," he said. "You'll be rewarded, dear heart."

He smiled, as if knowing full well how much the words hurt me.

After he had left and I was alone with the sleeping snake, I recovered my journal from the nightstand and curled in a corner where I began to write a story of when the world new, wondrous, and filled with monsters.

CHAPTER NINE

I HAD FINALLY fallen asleep when the creature jolted awake, its body thrashing as if in the throes of a grand mal seizure. Unsure, I pressed the damp cloth against him, my motherlike tenderness a poor imitation.

"It's okay. It's okay," I whispered to him.

The snake heaved, eyes widening as it stirred in place.

"They left me," he whimpered.

I started dabbing him again with a damp washcloth.

"They told me they never would," he said.

"What happened?"

The snake scanned me, as if assessing whether or not he could trust me. I simpered quietly, amused at the thought of a snake appreciating trustworthiness.

"We lost our home in the last airstrike," he explained. "My mother and father decided we should come here. Because they heard some of the places were vacant. Now that most of the families have left."

I pressed the bandage against his wound. He winced.

"Not all of us," I reminded him.

"But when I woke up…I called for them. I couldn't find them," he said, shivering. "I searched the whole nest they had made. They took my brothers. And my sisters. But they left me. They left me on purpose."

He turned away from me, choking on quiet sobs.

I collected the cloth and the bucket of water. Just as I rose from my knees, his head swiveled back to me.

"You won't leave, will you?" he asked.

I hesitated, unsure how to answer. "I'll stay."

I glanced away from him, hoping to hide the look that would tell him I really didn't want to.

"I'm Samael," the snake said. "What's your name?"

"Mara."

His face seemed to soften. "Thank you, Mara," he said.

I felt my cheeks heating red.

"I wish I could let go on purpose," I said.

I noticed Samael's face scrunched, bewildered.

"I'm sorry," I said, burying my face in my hands. "I shouldn't have said it. It's horrible to even think."

"What is it?" he asked me.

"If you hold on to a rope long enough, it'll pull you with it," I told him. "I've been holding on to one my whole life."

I sensed my eyes widening with horror, surprised at my own words. I pushed hair to cover my face, hiding.

"I'm sorry. I shouldn't have..." My voice trailed off.

"No. It's fine," Samael assured me.

I softened slightly, pulling threads of hair out of my face.

"I had a brother I never met," I told him. "He died—the same day I was born. Sometimes it feels like...he died just so I could live. And I've held on to that. I think I always will."

I noticed Samael staring at me, my reflection quivering in his dark eyes.

"Can I ask you something?" he asked me.

I nodded, unsure.

"What are you afraid of?" he asked. "Letting go, or being left with nothing to hold?"

I thought for a moment, considering how to answer.

However, before I could, we heard a crash from the next room. Samael shot up from bed, nervous.

"What was that?"

I tended to him, forcing him back beneath the sheets.

"Go back to sleep," I said to him.

After pulling a sheet over him and making certain he would not budge, I moved to a corner of the room where a large wooden board had been attached to the paneling. I pulled some out of the nails and lifted the board, revealing a small tunnel—a maze of narrow corridors, partitioned from the rest of the apartment with flimsy paneling. Some of the hidden pathways were exposed, with small holes ventilating the walls.

I crawled down the cramped passage, sensing one of the boards beneath my feet loosen. I pressed down and the board slid out, revealing a small empty chute no more than five feet deep. Dragging the board to cover the small chute, I crawled forward. Slowing as I reached a small outlet disguised with plywood, I slid the board away and peered into the living room. It was then I saw them—Rake and my mother. Bound together in a permanent embrace. Rake's legs—eight thin tree-like branches—swallowed my mother's naked body as they pressed against one another.

I watched, covering my mouth, as I saw Rake push my mother's middle finger inside his mouth, his fangs teasing the white thread tied around her finger. My mother convulsed, groaning, as if possessed. Rake tightened, his body fastening against hers. Then one of his legs slid down her pregnant stomach until the tip poked her belly button.

His eyes snapped to me as I watched, mouth unfolding and eyes flashing an invitation at me.

I didn't hesitate. I pushed the board over the outlet and retreated down the cramped corridor, sliding back into my bedroom. I flew out of the wall, my hands trembling.

Samael stirred beneath the sheets, uncoiling.

"What is it?" he asked.

I didn't answer him. Instead, I hastened to the nightstand beside the bed and blew out the candles.

"Go to bed," I ordered him.

I scurried to the corner and removed a large wooden board from the wall, exposing another hollow pocket in the paneling.

Ducking my head, I tucked myself inside the crawlspace. I dragged the board shut, casketing myself.

Crouching there with arms hugging my legs, I merely waited for daylight—for a deliverance that I knew would never come.

CHAPTER TEN

DAYLIGHT CREPT BENEATH the edges of the plywood covering the small crawlspace where I had spent the night. I pried my eyes open, wiping out the crust from the corners. Pushing the plywood aside, I crawled out of the wall as if I were mere vermin and skirted into my bedroom, where I found my mother kneeling beside Samael and offering him a small plate of food. They both seemed to pass soundless words to one another, none the wiser that I had joined them.

I stirred, tucking myself in the corner. I lifted my head and unfolded my arms, rubbing my eyes as I yawned. I watched as my mother gazed at the giant snake lying in my bed. She touched him, laughing.

"I had to stop myself," she said to him. "I almost called you... You act so much like my son. It's his birthday tomorrow—"

I watched Samael force a polite smile. Then, his head swiveled to me.

"Are you hungry?" he asked me.

"That food is for you, dear heart," my mother insisted, pushing the plate toward him. "You need your strength. No sharing."

I lifted myself off the damp floor, my pajamas wet and dripping.

"Is there any more bread?" I asked.

"This was the last of it," my mother said, her eyes glued to Samael as she watched him eat.

I sensed a dull ache in the pit of my stomach. "That was supposed to last us the rest of the month," I said.

"Well, you'll just have to go out and find more," my mother said, flashing a dangerous grin at me. "Won't you?"

I watched as my mother picked a piece of food off the plate and fed it to Samael. It was then I noticed her middle finger had been severed, the tip now dressed in the same bandages as her index finger.

"Your finger," I said, pointing.

My mother lurched off the floor, snarling at me like a wild dog. "And yours? I know exactly what you do with yours. I hear you at night. That's why you bite your nails, isn't it?"

I recoiled, my cheeks warming red.

"I hope you stayed away from it," she whispered to Samael. "Not for chastity's sake. The smell. What fifteen-year-old girl doesn't know how to wash their own cunt?"

Hissing at me, she stormed out of the room and disappeared.

I lowered my head, hiding my face from Samael. Shivering, my hands touched my mouth as I bit my lip. I sat on the edge of the bed, my arms tucked around my waist as if I were trying to make myself as small as possible.

I glanced over and noticed Samael pushing the plate of food toward me—a small offering.

I looked at him for a moment. Then, broke off a small piece of bread to snack on.

When I was finished eating, I ambled over to the sheet covering my bedroom door. I peeled it back, gazing into the living room.

I watched as my mother knelt, collecting bits of shattered glass into a small bucket. I saw Rake observing from the corner, as if he were a landowner supervising a mere serf.

Suddenly, as if summoned by him without words, my mother abandoned her chore and knelt before the giant spider. She buried her face in him, gagging on uncontrollable sobs. I found myself struggling to understand, leaning out further.

I watched as Rake lifted my mother's chin to meet his gaze. Then, he pressed his mouth against her eyes, draining the dampness from them. He pulled her face into his abdomen, claws cupping the back of her head.

When she was finished, he rose. Pecked her forehead with a kiss. Then he scampered from the room.

I lowered the sheet, retreating into my bedroom, where I hastened to a small chair set in the corner of the room. I grabbed a pair of jeans and hoisted them up about my waist.

"Where are you going?" Samael asked, stirring at the noise.

I answered him with a look of disgust. "Look. I'm sorry—for what happened to you," I said. "Your family. But I want you gone when I get back. The both of you."

Before he could respond, I flew out of the room and down the hallway into the nursery. Wading into the room, sewage lapped at my ankles. I approached my father's corpse lying on the mattress.

Kneeling on the bed beside the body, I removed the white cloth from his face. His ashen, expressionless mask greeted me.

I winced at the sight, my eyes threatening with tears.

"Come back," I whispered to him.

Just as I was about to reach for his hand, something troubled me. I sensed my face crumple with bewilderment as a small fly buzzed my head. I swatted it away.

Somehow, my father's arm beneath the bedsheet appeared to be shorter.

Without hesitation, I pulled back the sheet and a dark cloud of black flies swarmed in the air, humming at me. I coughed, covering my mouth when I finally saw the gruesome sight—my father's hand had been severed. The white of his exposed bone—a gorgeous pearl jeweled in a sleeve of tendon.

I searched his body, my gaze traveling until I found a dark stain blooming on the mattress where his left foot once was.

I hurled myself from the bed, doubling over and vomiting into my hand.

Unable to catch my footing, I staggered back and fell into the water. I scampered to my feet finally and darted out of the room.

I sailed down the hallway and into the bathroom, where I was greeted by Rake as he hung beside the bathroom mirror.

"Dear heart," he bellowed, grinning as if pleased by the sight of my discomfort. "Privacy is such an unnecessary commodity."

I watched as he descended from the mirror and scurried to the floor.

"We have no secrets from one another," he said to me.

I shrank from him, wiping the strands of saliva from my mouth. "I need to use the bathroom."

"That's all?" he asked, cornering me.

I clutched my stomach, doubling over. "I feel…sick."

"Of all the exquisite sufferings," the spider said. "A simple malady. The most ordinary and insignificant."

I pushed my hand against the door, hoping it might startle him. "Please. Leave."

"Not before I get what I want," he said, his fangs curling at me.

"What about what I want?" I asked. "You promised me. My father—"

He retreated slightly. "All good things to those who wait," he said.

"I'm done waiting," I told him. "You said you'd bring him back."

"When you give me what I want," the giant spider whispered.

He curled one of his legs at me, about to touch my face, when my mother appeared in the doorway.

"No," she said.

Rake turned, visibly upset he had been caught. "No?"

My mother moved in between the two of us, guarding me from the spider. "She's not ready," she said to him. "Not yet."

Rake simmered, about to explode. "Then when?" he demanded.

"Soon," my mother said, comforting him. "I promise."

Rake exhaled violently. Then, relaxing, he squinted at me. Just then, a flash of crimson flitted into the bathroom. Kali landed on Rake, chirping. The giant spider seemed to soften, amused.

"Mara. I told you to put her in the cage," my mother said.

I swiped at Kali, but Rake pulled her away as if far too devastated to part with the small red canary.

"What a beautiful creature," he said, admiring her.

"She was a gift," my mother explained. "From Mara's father."

I watched as Rake stretched out one of his limbs while the little canary stirred happily in place.

"There was a little boy I once met. I called him…Dismal Danny," Rake began. "Danny didn't like the way his father treated his mother. Especially when he had been drinking. Every night he'd listen to the same sounds. The sound of empty bottles hitting the wall. His mother screaming. Crying. So, one day, after debating the matter with his pet finch, Oscar, Dismal Danny decided to kill his father. He took the shotgun from the shed and waited in his room. But when the door opened and he finally shot, he saw his mother standing there. A dot of blood flowered between her eyes."

I watched as Rake's pincers snapped at the canary, the bird scaling the creature's leg.

"But she wasn't dead yet. So Dismal Danny took care of her," Rake said. "He dressed her wounds as best he could. Cared for her better than a husband. He wondered when his father would come back. Still waited for him. Never realized his mother had left him in the basement with a knife in his stomach and a plastic bag over his head. 'You have to finish what you started,' I said. And how did he respond? 'You can't help me.' There it was. That same invitation. I asked him, 'What's the one thing you love as much as your mother?' I already knew the answer. His pet finch, Oscar. So I showed him a trick. I ripped the bird apart in front of him. Tore every feather off. Bird soup sticking to my mouth in shiny red bits. 'You said it was a trick,' Danny said. I answered him, 'But it was, dear heart. You let go and let me hurt something you truly loved. Now. Your turn.'"

Before I could spoon Kali from Rake's leg, Rake seized the small bird and ripped her in half. I screamed, covering my mouth, as I watched the spider release his grasp, small bits of the bird sliding from his claws and crumpling onto the floor.

I knelt, scooping the remains into my palm.

"When will you let go, dear heart?" Rake asked me.

With that, he glided out of the bathroom and down the hallway.

I looked to my mother, as if begging her for a look of sympathy. She ignored me, shadowing Rake until she, too, disappeared with him.

I ambled from the bathroom into my bedroom, cradling the remains of my dead canary. I noticed Samael uncoil from the nest he had made of my mattress.

"What happened?" he asked me, stirring from his sleep.

I wouldn't even look at him. "I told you. I wanted you gone."

"Are you hurt?" he asked me.

I ignored him, splashing through the rising water as I marched toward Kali's birdcage. I opened the small door and pushed the canary's lifeless body inside.

Samael slithered toward me, his eyes immediately locating Kali's little corpse. "What happened?"

I shook my head, words impossible for the moment as if my tongue had been seized and plucked by its root. "There's something wrong with my mother," I said. "She's...changing."

I watched Samael search Kali's lifeless body as if for an explanation.

"Do you have a shoe box?" he asked me.

I wiped the wetness from my eyes. "What?"

"Something to bury her in."

"And put where?" I asked.

"She wouldn't want to stay in there," he said.

I ran my fingers up and down the length of the metal bars of Kali's birdcage. He was right—she certainly wouldn't want to stay trapped in there forever.

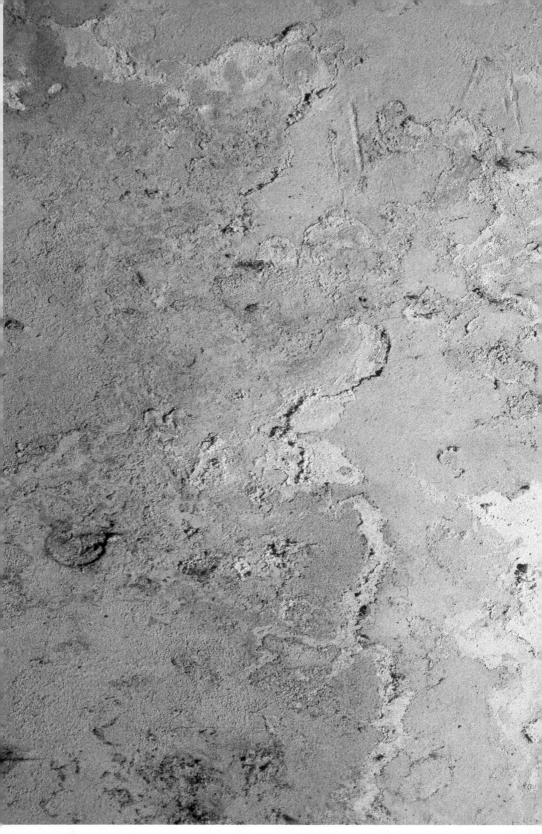

CHAPTER ELEVEN

WE GATHERED BESIDE the bed like respectful mourners, arranging a child's shoe box where we had placed Kali's body inside. I noticed Samael eyeing me, as if waiting for an instruction I wasn't prepared to give.

"Would you like to…?" he asked, his voice trailing off.

"No." I folded my arms. "I can't."

Of course, what I really meant was I didn't want to.

Samael merely nodded, seeming to understand. "It's okay."

I waited a few moments. The room stilled with silence, as if a giant cobweb had been draped over the two of us.

"My father…gave her to me the same day we went to the circus," I told him. "I was upset because we had missed seeing the Russian polar bears ice skating. So he bought her for me. Hid her in one of my shoe boxes. He surprised me when we got home. Ten days old. As pink as a newborn. Little white feathers like balls of cotton. She could balance on two of my fingers."

I closed my eyes, biting my lip. "When my father…"

I couldn't bring myself to say it—the word *death* becoming something gangrenous and vile that seemed to flower more and more every day despite my ignorance.

"I thought, 'At least I still have a part of him. Something he gave me.' I thought, 'I won't have to say goodbye yet.'"

I noticed Samael's mouth hanging open, his tongue flicking out and tasting the air. "I'm sorry," he said.

I shifted, unsure how to accept his compassion.

"Why are you being so nice to me?" I asked.

"You lost something," he said. "Like me."

I shook my head in disbelief. "But. The things I said to you—"

"You didn't mean them. Did you?"

I clutched an invisible wound in my stomach, Samael's kindness too much for me to bear.

"I did," I whispered to him, ashamed to admit it.

"Still do?" the snake asked.

I hesitated, uncertain. "I just want things to go back. To the way they were."

I watched Samael soften as if seeming to understand. "Where should we put...your friend?" he asked, eyeing the shoebox.

I looked around the room, my eyes finding the answer: the hollow hole in the paneling.

I gathered the shoe box in my arms and marched to the wall as if I were leading a funeral procession. I knelt beside the crawlspace, my fingers rubbing the box with a final farewell. Then, before another moment of hesitation, I pushed the small box inside the wall, casketing it forever.

"At least it's not a cage," I said to Samael, eyeing him, hopeful he would agree.

"I'd be thankful," Samael replied. "He's done far worse."

My eyebrows arched, studying him. I wondered if I had heard him correctly. "Who?"

Samael stammered, embarrassed, as if he had been caught.

"You mean... Rake?" I asked, searching his face for the truth.

Samael's guilt-filled eyes confessed the answer to me: "Yes," they seemed to say.

"How do you know?" I asked, backing away from him.

Samael hesitated, reluctant to answer.

"We used to work together," he explained, deflating. "I helped him with his act."

I recoiled until I was pressed against the wall. "You know him?"

"I didn't think I should tell you," the snake told me. "He didn't want you to know."

I was afraid to ask. "Know what?"

"That he invited me here. For you."

My mind raced, my vision starting to blur. Before I began to teeter, I lunged at Samael and spat in his face.

"I don't know what the fuck you two are planning. But I want you out," I shouted at him. "He can't bring my father back."

Before he could respond, I bolted out of my bedroom and down the hallway into my mother's room. Water seeped through the open doorway, a current of sewage swirling across the floor.

I tiptoed inside the empty room, uneasy. My eyes scanned every corner—draped and glistening with freshly spun silk webs. I examined my mother's empty bed. Then I moved across the room to the small window boarded shut with plywood. Peering outside, I saw nothing but an empty street.

Moving toward my mother's closet, I opened the door and began sifting through the hanging clothes. I lifted myself onto the tips of my toes, reaching up to the shelf as my hands moved small boxes.

Suddenly, a small rat scurried across my hand, squealing.

I let out a soft cry, falling back and dragging boxes with me as I tumbled. Papers and photographs scattered everywhere as they crashed to the sewage-soaked floor. I grabbed at the mess, stuffing everything back into boxes.

It was then I paused, coveting a small photograph I held in my hand. My face wrinkled, confused. The photograph—my mother, thirty years younger. I scanned the image as I saw her sitting upright in a hospital bed, her delighted smile almost rendering her unrecognizable as she cradled a newborn. But her happiness wasn't the most peculiar thing about the photo. It was the small child she was holding. His face—obscured with a dark reddish birthmark. Just like my father's.

I shifted slightly, the hairs on the nape of my neck rising as I sensed a presence stirring behind me.

As I turned, I was greeted by my mother in the doorway.

"What are you doing in my room?" she asked.

I swallowed hard, struggling to invent an excuse. I watched as my mother's eyes drifted from me to the small boxes bobbing in the sewage at my feet.

"You were going through my things?" she asked.

I answered, shoving the photograph at her. "Is this you?"

I watched as my mother squinted, studying the picture. Then she merely smiled.

"You can keep it," she said, pushing past me and kneeling to collect the boxes.

"That...thing you invited," I began, hounding her. "Samael knows him."

My mother wouldn't look at me, stuffing damp photographs into the boxes. "Yes."

"You knew that?"

My mother merely simpered, as if finally pleased I knew the truth. "I wasn't the only one who invited him," she said to me. "You have a hand in this too."

My eyes were glued to my mother, searching her face for an answer.

"When my mother died, my father welcomed sadness," my mother said. "Cleaning him out like a comb until he had changed."

I watched as her hands wandered below her waist. Between her legs.

"I gave myself to him," she explained. "To wipe the sadness from him. Until it was a stain."

"Why are they here?" I asked.

"They're here to help us," my mother said. "They promised me. Just like you promised me something."

I sensed myself withdrawing, like a child who had just broken an expensive family heirloom.

"I told you. Things would change," my mother said. "They're supposed to. Grief touches us differently. It's something we could've gone through together. The way it was meant to be. But. You ran."

I watched my mother search my face, as if she were squeezing out the very last ounce of resistance from me.

I buckled, defeated, until I began to sob quietly.

"I'm scared," I told her.

My mother merely grimaced at me. "We could've been scared together," she said.

"Everything's changing. It'll never be the same."

I noticed my mother's eyes hinting at something horrible.

"It's not supposed to," my mother said. "I never treated my father the way you treat me. I was all he had after my mother died. I was happy to be his. That's what a daughter is supposed to do. Things could've gone differently. If you didn't hate me so much."

"You think I hate you?" I asked her in disbelief.

My mother merely folded her arms, turning away from me.

"I don't hate you," I told her. "I'm just…scared."

I noticed my mother seemed to soften. She pulled a small silk thread from her pocket and approached me.

"I know," my mother said.

My mother wrapped both arms around me. I squirmed as if I were helpless prey being squeezed to death by a constrictor.

"But you won't be forever," my mother said to me. "I want you and me to go through this the way we're supposed to. Together."

"I want them to leave," I said, my voice cracking as I pleaded.

"They will," she told me, pecking my forehead with a kiss. "Once we give them what they want."

I pulled away from her, afraid to ask. "What do they want?"

"We have to make sacrifices," she told me. "Little ones. And then, it'll be over. They're going to help us. I promise."

Just then, Rake appeared at the doorway.

I shrank at the sight of him.

My mother grabbed hold of me, pushing me toward the giant spider and presenting me as if I were a sacrifice.

"Mara has had a change of heart," my mother explained to the impatient creature. She unspooled the thread and wrapped it around my index finger. "She's willing and ready."

Rake grinned so widely it looked as though his face might split in half.

"Like a happy family now," the spider said.

He reached out to touch me when we heard the sound of unfamiliar voices drifting in from the living room.

"Hello? Anyone home?" the voice asked.

Rake straightened. He softened at the sound of a voice he looked as if he had been expecting. Without a second thought, he scurried out of the room.

I looked to my mother with a question. There was no answer from her.

Following my mother into the living room, we came upon Rake as he idled over the large crack in the floor. Sewage water continued to pool around the hole, draining.

"Come quick," he said. "We have friends in need, dear hearts."

He kneeled, several of his legs disappearing beneath the floorboards to pull someone—something—up. An unfamiliar figure emerged—a giant lizard. The creature's giant body was a glimmering mosaic of flat plates and scales. The lizard stirred, tail thrashing and armored backside of horns flexing. Hind legs, sharp talons unfurling, grasped on the floor as the creature climbed through the small hole. The lizard glared at me with dark yellow eyes.

Once the lizard had fully surfaced, Rake knelt and pulled from beneath the floor another unfamiliar guest—a giant cockroach. Antennas quivering with excitement, the giant insect's forelegs buckled as he crawled out of the floor. He lunged forward, his amber-washed shell revealing two thin veined sheets of wings threatening to fly.

"Who are they?" my mother asked, shrinking away and plugging her nose at their stench.

"Dearest family members from my performing days," Rake explained.

He pointed to the lizard. "This is Lola." Then, gestured to the cockroach. "And this is Pitchfork. They've travelled a long way to see you."

"They…came to see us?" my mother asked, as if enchanted by the prospect of visitors clamoring to see her.

I watched as Lola, the giant lizard, flicked out her tongue to smell me and my mother.

"Are we allowed here?" Lola hissed.

My mother looked hesitant, as if wondering how to send them away with politeness.

I watched as Rake pressed his mouth against my mother's ear. He wrapped one of his bristled legs around her throat.

"Isn't my family always welcome, dear heart?"

My mother collected herself, forcing a smile.

"Yes. Of course," she said to him before turning to Lola and Pitchfork. "You're both very welcome here."

I immediately pulled on my mother's sleeve. "No," I said.

My mother shirked away. "Mara, what did I tell you?" she asked.

I grimaced, watching as the giant cockroach investigated the living room like a stray dog.

"Please excuse my daughter," my mother said to Lola and Pitchfork.

I began to back away, but Rake appeared behind me and ushered me toward our new houseguests. His mouth pushed against my ear, his breath heating my neck.

"You'll adore my friends, dear heart," he assured me.

The cockroach stirred, excited, as Rake pushed me toward him. I resisted as much as I could, trembling.

"I think the little bitch is scared," Lola said, laughing.

Rake released me, his eight eyes narrowing at Pitchfork with a scrupulous gaze—an inspector keen on answers.

"Have you been giving him food?" he asked Lola.

She lowered her head, hiding a look of guilt. "No," she said. "I promise."

Rake's eyes went over the giant cockroach, examining his every inch. "He looks as healthy and full as a sow in a slaughterhouse."

Without warning, Rake slammed one of his legs into the large insect. Pitchfork cowered, afraid.

"I swear. I haven't," Lola assured him.

Rake wrapped a leg around the lizard, threatening to squeeze. "It would be humiliating to be proved a liar by a small coil of his shit. Wouldn't it, dear heart?"

Lola merely blinked, nervous. "He hasn't eaten. I promise."

Rake finally released her, turning to my mother and me. "You both are very lucky," he said to us. "These are two of the most exceptional performers. Lola especially."

I watched as my mother studied the giant lizard, bewitched.

"Beautiful," my mother exhaled.

"Beauty's not her only talent," Rake explained, and then gestured to Lola. "Show her, dear heart."

Lola, seeming always too delighted to oblige, crawled toward my mother. Rake motioned for my mother to kneel, and she obeyed. Lola met her at eye level. Then, without a single word, she dragged her massive tongue across my mother's face. When she was finished, Lola backed away from her, tongue sliding across her lips to taste.

"Your greatest fear...is standing in this room with you right now," the lizard said. "Is that right?"

My mother stammered, unsure, and looked to me as her cheeks heated red.

"I didn't... I think..."

Rake, always too delighted to put my mother out of her misery, intervened as was his custom. "You don't have to answer, dear heart," he said. "Lizards have an exemplary sense of smell. Especially with their tongues."

Pitchfork thrashed on the ground.

"And her friend?" my mother asked, gesturing to the giant cockroach.

"The 'crown jewel' of our performance," Rake explained. "He served a very special purpose. Still does."

"What is it?" my mother asked.

"He'll show you. But, for now, they need their rest," Rake said, glaring at my mother as if insulted she hadn't offered. "Don't you agree?"

"Yes. Of course," my mother said, gesturing for Lola and Pitchfork to follow her down the hallway toward the nursery.

But I immediately blocked their path.

"We don't have any room," I said.

"Mara. Be quiet," my mother said, shooing me away. Then she turned to Rake. "They can stay in the nursery."

"No. They can't," I said, stomping my foot like a toddler throwing a tantrum.

"Is there something wrong?" Lola asked my mother.

I watched as my mother cleared the catch in her throat, her eyes lowering as if avoiding Lola's question.

"My husband," she began, "he passed—two days ago."

Pitchfork scurried to my feet, smelling me. I jerked my leg, scaring him and splashing him with water. The giant insect immediately flinched and retreated.

"They're not staying in there," I said, folding my arms. "That's his room."

My mother eyed me with a look of hatred. "Mara—"

"We don't need much space," Lola assured her, gesturing to the sofa.

I watched as my mother shook her head, humiliated.

"I'm sorry," she said. "The couch is comfortable. I promise."

CHAPTER TWELVE

IT WAS LATE at night when Lola and Pitchfork finished performing for us on the small stage we had built in the living room. Occasionally glancing away from their performance, my eyes wandered across the room to where my mother and Rake were seated on the sofa. She massaged one of his legs, mesmerized by their showmanship. I rolled my eyes, hugging my legs against my chest and curling into an armchair to write in my journal.

When they were finally finished, my mother jumped to her feet and applauded.

"Magnificent as always," Rake exclaimed, visibly pleased. "You've been rehearsing."

Lola and Pitchfork bowed.

It was then my mother noticed me lost in my writing, as usual.

"Mara. You're being rude to our guests again," she said to me before glancing back at Lola and Pitchfork. "I'm sorry. She wastes all day writing these...stories."

"She's creative," Rake said, flashing a hideous grin at me. "Kindred spirits."

"Will you let us read one?" Lola begged, scurrying toward me and tongue flicking out.

I closed my notebook, pressing it tight against my chest. "It's not finished yet."

My mother flashed me a look: *liar*. "You let me read it already," she said.

"Won't you share it, dear heart?" Rake begged.

"We won't judge," Lola assured me, wiping her tongue across her lips.

Pitchfork scampered to my feet, his eyes begging me. I ignored the pathetic creature. Instead, my eyes fastened to Rake.

"If you honor your end of the deal," I said to him.

"Deal?" my mother asked, head swiveling to the giant spider. "What deal?"

My eyes burned holes in Rake. "He knows."

"First, a story," he said. "Then the magic, dear heart."

My mother rose from her seat, glaring at me.

"I'll tell a story," she said.

Lola and Pitchfork scampered along the carpet to sit while my mother climbed the small performance area to address the entire room. She faced us, her speaking uneasy. Her eyes avoided me at all costs.

"It's about a mommy who had a beautiful baby boy. Skin as smooth as velvet. His hair—as soft as cotton," she said. "A mouth that always smiled. Perfect—in every way. And Mommy said to Daddy, 'Now that I have him, I'll never love you as much as I love him.' So Daddy tried to prove her wrong, and he did. Because—she got pregnant again. She didn't want to be pregnant. She had her perfect baby. She didn't need another. So she tried to get rid of it. But it didn't work. When you're given a gift, something else gets taken away. The perfect little baby boy—was taken away. And all she was left with was a child—a baby girl—she didn't want."

I winced slightly, my eyes watering. I knew exactly who she was talking about.

"It was then—Daddy said to Mommy, 'Now that I have her, I'll never love you as much as I love her.' But Mommy was going to prove him wrong."

Finally, my mother's eyes found me. A look of loathing—unbridled disgust.

"Thank you, dear heart," Rake said. "Won't you sit?"

I watched as my mother returned to her seat, her face hardening with an immovable mask of hatred.

Rake scaled the large web curtaining the wall.

"Perhaps you'd all like to see one of my favorite acts?" he said. "This was always a crowd pleaser. Especially with the little ones."

He eyed Samael. "Would you help me?"

Samael glanced at me, and then at Rake. He uncoiled from his nest, slithering toward the giant spider.

I couldn't bear it anymore. I lurched out of my seat and hastened down the hallway into the bathroom. I went to lock the door when I discovered that the latch had been broken. Too upset to care, I pushed myself against the sink. Both of my hands braced the rim of the bowl. I lowered my head, my breathing heavy and broken.

I turned on the sink faucet and it sputtered a cough—no water.

Lifting my head, I wiped my eyes and met my reflection in the mirror.

Suddenly, there was a scratching sound at the door.

"Go away," I shouted.

More scratching. This time, dangerous.

I grabbed the handle and flung the door open. There, I was greeted by a dark shape squatting on the floor—Pitchfork.

The insect stirred, antennas brushing against my feet and gliding up my ankle with an obscene proposal. I jolted away, disgusted.

"Stay away from me," I told him.

I slammed the door shut with a thud.

Returning to the sink, my solitude was short-lived when the door flew open again. It clapped against my legs, and I cried out, my knees buckling.

Pitchfork crawled into the bathroom. I shrank into a corner as he approached.

"Get out of here," I shouted to him.

I watched as the insect began to size me up and down, antennas bending at me with a proposition. One of his legs brushed against mine. I winced, distrustful at first. But it wasn't long before his gentleness relaxed me.

When he recognized my resolve easing, he pounced. Legs coiled around me, tightening.

I screamed, fighting him off.

Pitchfork crawled over me, his antennas taunting me as they frisked me. I resisted, slipping on the wet floor and slamming my face into the mirror. The glass cracked like an eggshell. My hands flailed, grabbing at the sink as I sobbed uncontrollably.

Pitchfork tightened his limbs around me, mounting my head as I slammed into the glass once more. The mirror exploded. Glittering shards of glass scattered in the sink.

With all the force I could gather, I pushed Pitchfork off me. The insect careened back, skating across the tiled floor. I swiped a long shard of glass in the sink and lunged for the door, crying. But his legs were already at my neck as he threw himself onto me.

I swiveled and, with a single blow to decide the matter, I drove the shard of glass into him.

Pitchfork halted. His eyes widened, surprised. His legs twitched.

He opened his mouth, revealing the glistening dagger skewering his head.

I watched him as he staggered back, legs giving way before he fell and crashed against the toilet with a vulgar thud. He curled there like a puppet.

My eyes never left his body. I opened my mouth to scream, but there was no sound.

Before I could move, the door swung open to reveal my mother, Rake, and Samael at the threshold.

"What happened?" the giant spider asked.

He finally saw Pitchfork—a crumpled heap piled on the floor.

Scurrying past me, Rake crouched beside his body.

"What have you done?" he asked.

I watched as my mother noticed the colorless blood drooling from Pitchfork's open mouth, panic flooding her face.

"What the fuck have you done?" she cried, shaking me.

But I didn't feel anything. There was nothing to be felt. I looked down and noticed my hands—spattered with blood, twitching in involuntary spasms. My lips moved with soundless words. I glanced in the remnants of the bathroom mirror, my face shimmering with the small bits of glass glued to my reflection's skin.

I watched as Samael slinked toward Rake, tending to Pitchfork's body.

Rake wrapped Pitchfork's body with silk webbing, dragging him from the room by a glistening thread into the nursery, where we followed.

Rake arranged Pitchfork's swaddled body on the bed beside the sheet-draped corpse of my father, a swarm of flies blanketing my father's lifeless remains.

"Please. I didn't think she would ever..." my mother said, hounding Rake. "This was not something I ever thought of. Please don't—"

But Rake ignored her, too preoccupied with tending to Pitchfork's corpse.

I stood in the nursery's doorway, shaking with quiet sobs. I sensed Lola coiling her tail around my feet as if straining to remove me from the room, but I resisted.

"Get her the fuck out of here," my mother hollered at Lola.

I released a guttural groan, lunging at my mother as I wiped the blood from my forehead with trembling hands.

"Please. I have to get this off," I said, quivering as I presented my blood-soaked hands to her.

But my mother was far too concerned with Rake, hounding him and failing to get his attention.

"Please. Look at me," she begged him.

Rake swirled around, wrapping one of his legs around my mother's throat. He pressed his face against hers as she squirmed, nearly choking.

"This…changes everything," he said.

Flashing his fangs, he released her and leapt out of the room, where he disappeared. I watched as my mother doubled over, coughing and gasping for air.

"Please," I begged her. "Help me."

My mother wouldn't even look at me. Her voice was low and grating as if her throat were filled with gravel.

"Clean yourself," she said.

I looked around, nervously. "Where?"

My mother answered, eyeing the sewer pipe hanging from the wall.

Realizing it was my only option, I gagged on small whimpers as I eased my hands beneath the water dripping from the broken valve. The blood vanished from my hands. It was then I noticed my mother, Samael, and Lola were still watching me.

"Please," I begged them. "Don't look at me."

But they didn't react.

I sobbed, lowering my pants and lifting my shirt. Folding my arms to cover my breasts, I leaned in toward the leaking pipe again and grimaced at the horrible smell. Clutching my stomach, I vomited.

I watched as blood swirled down my naked body in dark ribbons—tiny threads that had forever come undone from me and were sent to freedom.

CHAPTER THIRTEEN

A FEW HOURS went by, and I was left alone in my bedroom until Samael coiled in the doorway, watching me as I dressed. He seemed to twitch faintly when I noticed him.

"Go away," I shouted.

Samael's eyes lowered, nervous. "He sent me."

I hoisted a pair of jeans around my waist, my eyes avoiding the snake at all costs.

"Leave," I said to him.

But he wouldn't.

"I believe you," he said, crawling into the room, and his throat tightening as he spoke.

"Believe?"

"It was an accident," he said.

But he didn't understand. It wasn't an accident. I had wanted to hurt something, just as he had hurt me when I uncovered his lie.

"Your family never left you," I said to him.

Samael's head lowered. "He came to me when I needed him most."

"We don't need him," I said, challenging the large snake as if I were prepared for a fight. "We never did."

"Your mother says you do."

I deflated for a moment.

"Please," I begged him. "Why won't you leave?"

"He's asking for you," Samael told me. "There are others coming."

I looked at him queerly. *Others?*

He recognized the bewilderment closing in around my eyes.

"Friends," he said. "To pay their respects."

I didn't wait another moment. I pushed past him, hastening into the living room, where I found the room had vanished beneath a tidal wave of vermin. Large rodents scurried, emerging from the hole in the floor. Giant cockroaches teemed along the walls, climbing down from the ledge opened in the ceiling.

Rake passed around the room with somber greetings. I watched as my mother flanked him, unbothered by the sight of pestilence and instead playing the role of the dutiful spouse.

Without hesitation, I tossed myself into the heaving throng of vermin. Searching their faces for an explanation, the uninvited guests answered me with violent hisses. A giant rat with blood-matted fur and a crumpled, half-torn left ear snarled at me as I passed. I ducked, startled, as a massive cockroach with a missing antenna and splintered casing unfurled his wings and flew at me.

I rubbed my eyes in disbelief as a large rat with a red scar covering his snout weaved between my legs, squealing. Finally mooring myself against the wall, I scanned the room and noticed several rodents snarling and fighting one another.

Giant lizards soon joined the chaos, their shimmering emerald bodies snaking through the shredded panels.

Rake—as usual—took command of the room, mounting his massive cobweb. The drone of the crowd weakened to a mere whisper as he scaled his perch.

Collecting his thoughts with a look of uneasiness, his brittle-thin voice wavered slightly. For the first time, he appeared unpoised.

"I wanted to thank you all for coming today," he said. "To remember…someone we all knew and loved."

I watched as Rake glanced at my mother—a crumbling pillar. She winced, doing all she could to hide a small tremor of pain. Clutching her stomach, she forced a polite smile.

"At this time, I'd like to invite anyone who may like to speak on the behalf of our departed brother," he said.

Rake searched the horde of animals for a volunteer. His eyes invited a rat with no front legs. The rodent replied, scared, lowering its head. He begged the rat with the half-torn ear with a mere look. No response.

I noticed my mother watching me as she stood beside Rake. I watched her swallow hard, her face heating with fury.

"I'd like to say something," she said.

Rake agreed, withdrawing, as my mother took the stage.

My mother addressed the crowd. She did not tremble. Instead, she spoke with a rehearsed conviction. Everything Rake had taught her of showmanship—now on full display.

"These never get easier. Believe me," she said. "In fact, each one seems to take a larger piece of you. Until you're…"

Her voice trailed off—something she was going to say but didn't.

"I didn't know your friend," she said. "So I may not be the most fit to speak on his behalf. If anyone else wants to speak, you can stop me—"

She searched the crowd. There were no signs of objection.

"But. I understand pain. Your sorrow," my mother said. "I still feel it. It's the same pain I felt when my father died. When my husband died. When my son—"

She stopped again. Steadied her breathing.

"There's a reason for your pain," she said, her eyes narrowing at me and pointing. "And it's standing right there."

The horde of vermin shifted, facing me.

"She's the cause of your suffering," my mother said. "And I will not accept responsibility for it. What she did to your—"

My mother stopped herself from saying the word, trembling.

"She did the same thing to my son," she said. "He died in sacrifice. Just so that she could live."

I watched as my mother straightened, visible delight washing over her.

"That…thing is no longer my daughter," she said. "You can have her."

The swarm of vermin began to inch toward me. Cockroaches leapt to the wall, cornering me. Rats crawled to my feet, screeching.

"And what about what you did to my father?" I shouted at her. It was my only defense.

I watched as my mother turned away, Rake comforting her.

"I can't even look at her…" my mother said, burying her face into the spider's arm.

Before another animal came closer toward me, I lunged at my mother. The crowd parted as I barreled through.

"Show them what you've done to him," I said. "I want you to show them."

My mother wheezed, clutching her stomach.

"I want her gone," she said, begging Rake to act fast.

"How you kept his body here just so you could eat him," I screamed.

Suddenly, my mother doubled over, howling in agony. I saw the place between her legs begin to darken. She grabbed Rake, bracing herself. Another surge of anguish leveled her as her knees buckled and she cried out.

I recoiled, wondering if my words had somehow done this to her—if I had somehow willed this to happen. "Mother?"

Without hesitation, Rake mounted my mother, blanketing her body in a silk web. Then he dragged her toward the nursery.

The horde swarmed them.

One of the cockroaches wiped their antennas over my mother's body as they passed. A lizard clawed at her, chattering. Rake shooed them from his path.

"Out of the way," he shouted.

The vermin scattered at his mere command.

I began to elbow my way through the horde, struggling to catch up with Rake and my mother.

"Please," I wept. "Let me through."

Before I could be leveled again by a flying cockroach as it buzzed me, I knocked into Samael.

"Follow me," he shouted.

The swarm separated as he bulldozed through them and into the nursery, where Rake had already pushed Pitchfork's corpse off the mattress. The body slid from the bed and onto the floor with a splash. I covered my mouth as I saw my father floating there too—lying face-down beside the bed like waste.

I watched as Rake spread my mother out onto the bed, ripping the silk webbing from her. She writhed, screaming in agony.

"We want to see," one of the rodents shouted as more began to crowd into the nursery.

The pack of vermin followed him. Samael struggled to keep them out, but they slipped past him.

"Please," another rodent begged. "Let us watch."

"Get out," I screamed at the uninvited guests as I rushed to my mother's side.

I looked at Rake, pleading for him to do something—anything. He remained unmoved.

Watching one of the large rodents mount the bed, I saw the creature crouch in front of my mother as her legs were pried open. His snout disappeared where her legs met.

"Baby's coming," the rodent yelled.

Cockroaches swarmed the room, vaulting from wall to wall. One of the larger insects leapt on the bed, tossing me out of the way.

"The bitch has to push," it said.

The rat buried its snout between my mother's legs once more.

"Harder," the rodent shouted.

The horde began to teem around the bed, knocking me aside. I clawed at them, trying to push through the wall of vermin, but to no avail.

"Get away from her," I shouted.

Another cockroach landed on my mother's body, its legs frisking her as he examined.

"My, my," the insect said.

My mother's face flushed with panic. She released a cry of defeat.

"I can't do it," she screamed.

Rake hung above her, two of his legs cupping her face.

"It'll be over soon," he said. "I promise."

The rodent stirred, wading in blood as it pooled on the bed. His snout disappeared between my mother's legs once more.

"I see the head," he shouted.

The horde immediately answered, erupting in a frenzy.

Cockroaches flitted around the room. Rodents and lizards scampered across the floor, massive bodies slamming into one another as if in celebration.

I watched my mother shudder, screaming.

Rake pressed his mouth against her forehead. "Almost, dear heart," he whispered.

I watched as the horde of creatures began to swarm, disappearing in a blur until they seemed to move as one. Claws wrapped around legs. Wings beat against fur.

I watched Lola reclining on the bed beside my mother. Another lizard began to mount her, their tails entwining as they thrashed against her.

Rake mounted my mother's body, his legs furiously at work as glistening ropes of silk seemed to swallow her whole.

My mother pushed, screaming, for the final time when a small wet bundle slid out onto the mattress.

"Let me see," I shouted, elbowing my way through the pack. "Out of the way."

My mother—her body veiled with silk webbing—fell back against the mattress. Exhausted. One of the rodents began to circle the newborn, sniffing.

"It's a boy," he shouted to the others.

Eyes closing, my mother's breath hissed.

"Let me hold him," she whispered.

Rake wrapped the newborn with silk, passing the precious bundle to my mother. Her face softened as she nursed the child. I watched her wipe the fluid from the infant's blood-smeared face as it shifted against her chest. She pulled the baby closer.

"He's...perfect," she whispered.

I pushed to the front of the pack, finally reaching the mattress. My mother seemed to notice me, but didn't say anything.

Rake lunged at the child.

"Don't touch him," I said.

My mother scowled at me.

"I want to be alone now," she said, looking at Rake and, for the first time, commanding him to obey.

Rake rose, addressing the horde.

"Everyone out," he said. "Now."

With Samael's assistance, Rake ushered the vermin out of the room until all had disappeared. Only my mother and I remained.

I frowned, watching my mother's fingers tighten around the newborn.

"You screamed so much. I wondered if it hurt you more than it did me. It was as if you knew you had done something you could never take back," she said to me. "With that shit-eating smirk you practiced. I should've burned you in your cradle when I had the chance."

The small child mewled, twisting in his silk blanket.

"A boy gives things to his mother a daughter cannot," my mother explained. "Your father couldn't—wouldn't—give me things anymore. I blamed you for his leaving just to hurt you. The truth is—he left because I had already taken everything from him."

"What?"

My mother smiled, as if pleased by my blankness. "They were things a mother deserves to take from her son. But the things he gave you instead. The love. Should've been mine. He was the stain my father had marked me with."

It was then I finally understood.

"He was your *son*?"

Rake returned. I noticed my mother eye him, as if expectant.

"Is it—?"

He scaled the wall, scurrying across the ceiling until he hung above her by a single white thread.

"It's time, dear heart," he said.

My mother relaxed, as if prepared. A moment she had been waiting for. Releasing her grasp, Rake pulled the child from her arms.

"What are you doing with him?" I asked.

He carried the cobweb-swathed bundle to the small bassinet arranged in the corner of the room. Then he returned to my mother's side.

"Are you ready, dear heart?" he asked her.

My mother answered, smiling at him with an invitation.

I watched as Rake pressed his mouth against my mother's, a silent language passing through them. Pleased, as if his mouth had drained the very last bit of opposition from her, he mounted and restrained her.

She submitted to him, spreading her legs as Rake bound them with webbing.

Then, Rake opened his mouth, fangs glinting at me with a warning—a signal telling me, "You'll be next."

"No," I shouted at him.

Willing myself to move, I darted to the wall. A wooden board slid out to reveal another secret passage. I vanished inside, dragging the panel shut.

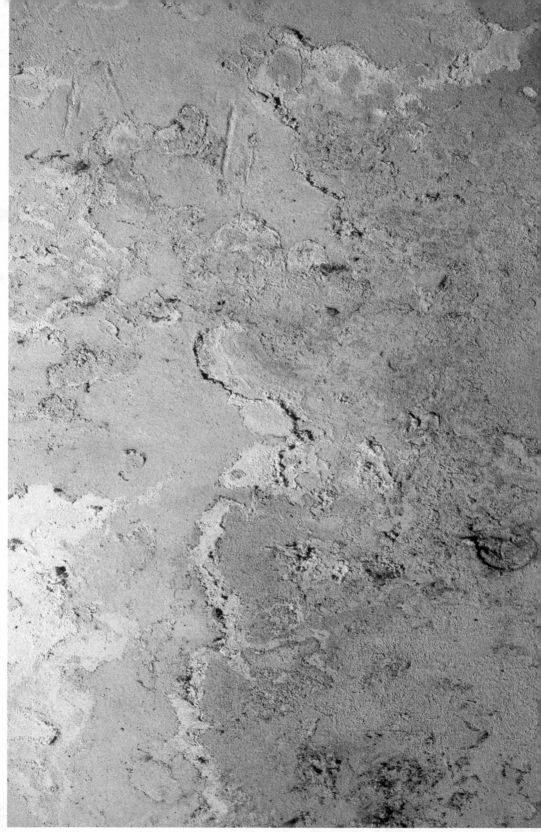

CHAPTER FOURTEEN

I CRAWLED DOWN the secret passageway, my ears perking at the dim chorus of shrieks and chirps echoing beyond the wall. Passing ventilated outlets where the paneling had been ripped open, I saw giant shadows of vermin flashing at me.

One of the panels at the end of the passage exploded, a giant cockroach sailing through the wall and crashing into the corridor. I reeled at the sight; my path was now blocked. I watched as the dazed insect stumbled back out through the gaping maw in the paneling.

It was then I noticed one of the ledgers had cracked apart, the splintered wood creating a giant spear. I hesitated to continue, the giant splinter aiming directly at me. But my feet made the decision to inch further down the passage as the muffled sounds of squealing grew louder.

I braced myself, squirming down the cramped corridor.

Suddenly, the wall exploded.

Wings and claws burst through the opening to seize me. I screamed, struggling as the creatures pulled at my hair and tore me from the passageway into the living room, where they finally released me. Lifting my head, I covered my mouth, and my eyes widened with horror at the sight— a feeding frenzy.

Cockroaches swarmed in giant waves, rats springing after them and ripping apart their extremities. Lizards zigzagged through the tide of vermin, their tongues stabbing the air and jaws seizing the smaller rodents.

I watched in horror as a rat lunged on a cockroach, teeth clamping down until the insect's armored shell split open with a wet crunching sound. Its face slimed with fluid, the rat buried its snout deep in the abdomen of its lifeless prey and gorged. I watched as a giant lizard ambushed another rat, jaws snapping shut around its helpless prey and the rodent finally exploding in a geyser.

I screamed, blood hosing my face as I watched the lizard shaking the rat back and forth until its lifeless body swung from the creature's mouth without movement. Rubbing my eyes in disbelief, I watched as another lizard caught a cockroach. Tongue shooting from its mouth, the reptile ladled the insect from the wall and ripped its head off.

I doubled over, vomiting in my hand, as the cockroach's head skated to my feet.

Just then, I saw Samael weaving through the crowd, fangs unfurled, as he hunted a smaller rat. I pushed toward him, calling out his name. He ignored me, stabbing the rodent with his mouth. The rat twitched until it slowed, paralyzed.

I watched as Samael stretched his jaw, preparing to feed.

"Please," I begged him. "Stop."

Samael whipped the dagger-like tip of his tail at my face, slicing my cheek open. I felt a small line of blood creep beneath my eyelid. He turned to me, realizing with a look of "What have I done?" As if severed from his trance-like primal state and horrified, he slithered toward me with a tender offer.

"I'm—" he began.

But I refused his proposition, scurrying away from him as I weaved through the feeding frenzy. I ran, pushing half-dead carcasses out of my way and dodging thrashing tails. I looked at the main entryway—the exit was blocked. A small horde of creatures ambushed prey near the plywood-covered front door.

Just then, a wave of rodents crashed into me and pushed me back into the nursery. I crashed to the floor with a splash. Spitting sewer water from my mouth, I lifted my head and saw Rake straddling my mother's naked body. His backside faced me; his unseen legs were busy at work. My knees buckling, I staggered to my feet and inched toward the bed.

Then, I finally saw it—Rake's mouth working through my mother's arm.

My mother—a lifeless effigy. Doll-like eyes stared heavenward, vacant, her lifeless body curtained with cobwebs. I noticed my father's naked corpse lying next to my mother. More parts of him had been eaten away.

Claws holding his lifeless prey, Rake pulled my mother's arm closer as he chewed. Blood rinsed his face as his mouth worked deeper, her muscle splitting apart as if it were merely damp cotton.

I found myself backing into a corner, unable to pull my eyes away.

Rake devoured faster, delighted to perform for an audience.

The very last threads of my mother's tissue loosened with a squelching sound. The arm finally separated. I screamed, covering my eyes.

It was then that the remaining animals swarmed the bed.

Rake presented the severed limb to them as if it were a sacred donation.

"When you're given a gift, something else gets taken away," he said to them.

Then, with the flick of his wrist, he tossed the arm at the crowd.

Two rodents caught the severed limb, fighting over it for a moment before finally scurrying off with their reward.

"Bring me the woman's daughter," Rake ordered.

One of the lizards coiled a tail around my arm, hauling me toward the mattress despite my pleading. I watched helplessly as Lola unfastened some of the silk webbing from my mother's legs and looped it around the dead woman's neck until it could be used as a garrote.

Rake grabbed me by the throat and forced me to straddle my mother's corpse. He slid the thin cable of webbing into my hands. It glistened in the candlelight as if it were made of metal.

I shivered, weeping.

"Please," I begged him. "Make this stop."

Rake pressed his mouth against my face, bristles tickling.

"It'll be over soon, dear heart," Rake said. "But first. You have to cut it off."

His words began to snake through my head in whispers.

"Cut it off," he repeated, until the animals began to chant the same thing too.

I looked around the room, my eyes watering, as the vermin closed in on me—their mouths snarling at me with the repeated command.

"CUT. IT. OFF."

Their chanting finally reached an unbearable crescendo.

Rake guided my hands as I pressed the wire against my mother's neck and began to saw. Wrenching with force, I winced at the shrill sound of the thread at work.

The horde continued to chant, their bodies spasming as if possessed.

I pulled the cord tighter, my mother's blood squirting my face.

"CUT. IT. OFF."

Finally, I did.

My mother's head severed, rolling forward in my lap. My hands buttered with blood, I loosened my grip about the thread of webbing corkscrewed like a pig's tail. I stared at my mother's headless body, my eyes unblinking and my mouth open in horror at the skill of my craftsmanship.

The horde of vermin flocked around the bodies, tearing the remains apart. They descended on my father's corpse, mouths pressing against his skin and ripping the gristle from the bone.

I screamed, swatting at them until one of the animals bit me. I finally slumped from the mattress, collapsing.

Rake immediately motioned for some of the pack members to apprehend me. I didn't resist this time as they held me. I was too tired to fight.

Eyelids threatening to close, my breath whistled. I whimpered, my head bobbing back and forth.

"Please," I said. "Will you go now?"

Rake pressed his mouth against my forehead, sucking off some of the blood.

"I can't," he said. "Not yet."

I sensed my body slackening, all hope draining out from me. "When?"

His mouth brushed against my ear, his breath heating my neck.

"When we're fed," he said.

Then, two rodents dragged the half-eaten remains of my mother and father from the mattress. Their lifeless bodies splashed, landing face-down in the water.

Rake pushed my body against the bed, roping my arms with thick cables of silk. I thrashed, screaming until I was hoarse.

Lola pinned me down, her claws squeezing my throat until I finally slowed without movement.

It was then the creatures began to resume their chanting—"CUT. IT. OFF."

Rake mounted me, eight legs swallowing me in a permanent embrace.

My eyes begged him with a final plea.

But he ignored it, burying his mouth against my arm as he began to feed.

CHAPTER FIFTEEN

I STIRRED AWAKE, heavy eyelids straining to open. I could feel my legs beating against tightening strings of silk webbing woven around my feet.

I rolled on my side, reminded of my missing right arm as I slumped in a puddle of my own blood.

I slid away from it, finding my empty sleeve had been fastened in a makeshift tourniquet.

I scanned the room and found Samael curled at the foot of my bed. He uncoiled, noticing I was awake.

"He's been waiting for you," he said.

I raked my head back against the pillow. There was no modicum of comfort to be found.

"Please," I begged him. "Help me."

"He wanted to take more," he said. "I told him to stop. He wrapped your sleeve to stop the bleeding."

"It hurts," I said, the agony pummeling my voice to a mere murmur.

Samael looked as if he knew, wishing he could do more.

"They'll want to know you're awake," he said. "They're going to be hungry again."

"Where are they?" I asked.

Samael eyed the door. "Outside. Sleeping."

"Can't you make them leave?" I asked him.

"And say what?"

"Anything," I told him.

"They won't leave without food," he replied.

I heard the newborn shifting in his bassinet, crying. My eyes began to water at the horrible reminder.

"There's something you could do," Samael said.

I dreaded his answer.

"Give them the child," he said.

I stared at him in disbelief. "What?"

"You can make a deal with them."

The newborn shrieked again, as if the infant somehow knew full well what Samael was proposing.

"Rake thinks he's owed something," Samael explained. "Then they'll leave. I promise."

I hesitated, closing my eyes and carefully considering his words.

"I...can't," I said to him.

"They'll kill you both."

I paused for a moment, thinking. I could scarcely believe the words I was about to say.

"They can have me instead."

Samael recoiled, surprised.

"Will you hide him?" I asked, gesturing to the newborn. "See to it they don't find him."

"Where?" he asked.

My gaze drifted to the sewage pipe hanging from the hole in the nursery's wall.

"There's a crawlspace behind that," I told him.

I lifted myself up, legs swinging over the side of the mattress. Leaning on Samael for support, I pushed down on the floor with both feet and finally ambled toward the bassinet arranged in the corner of the room.

Sparkling blue eyes swaddled in a blanket of webbing greeted me.

With my remaining arm, I leaned down and scooped up the infant. He stirred, cooing.

I staggered over to the leaking sewage pipe. Hoisting his little body through the opening, I lowered him down inside the half-ventilated crawlspace. I pulled the blanket over his face to muffle his cries, then tucked him beneath a wooden shelf.

Samael shifted at my side.

"I'll make sure they don't find him," he promised me.

My mouth creased with a smile—a wordless "thank you."

"They're waiting, you know," he said.

I thought for a moment. Suddenly, an idea. I ambled to the mattress. Greased my face with blood. I swallowed hard. Prepared for battle.

Without another moment to hesitate, I limped into the living room. Samael slithered close behind me.

I noticed the dark figures of cockroaches glued to the walls shifted, as if disturbed by the appearance of fresh, wounded prey. Lizards uncoiled their tails, stirring awake from the shallows of the damp floor. The snouts of rodents appeared in the holes of paneling—white teeth flashing and whiskers twitching.

I moved into the center of the room, scanning every corner for Rake.

I walked into him as he dangled from the ceiling by a thread.

"Dear heart," he said. "I thought we were going to have to practice persuasiveness with you. I'm delighted to see you're a willing participant."

He rubbed one of his legs along my face. I winced at his touch.

"You're eager," he said. "Sublime."

Rake, upside down, swung toward me. But I didn't back down.

"I'm yours," I told him.

"The child first," he insisted.

I approached him. "You can't," I said.

"No?"

"I ate him."

Rake recoiled, surprised, as he watched me wipe some of the blood from my mouth.

"I was his sister," I said. "I wanted to be the only one to hurt him."

The horde began to close in around me and Samael. Rake glared at me, doubtful.

I glanced to Samael for support. "Tell him."

The secret flashed between our eyes.

"I watched her," Samael said to Rake.

Rake descended from the silk cable, scampering to the floor with a violent thud. "Not close enough," he said.

Then he turned to address the horde.

"It seems we have an entirely different matter to settle, then," the giant spider announced. "A traitor in our midst. Death to turncoats."

I watched as lizards flicked their tongues at me. Rodents squealed as if preparing to attack.

I stood my ground. "I'm not afraid of you."

Rake merely laughed. "You will be."

Without warning, Rake swiped at Samael and sliced his underside open. As if commanded by a mere thought, the pack of vermin pounced on him to attack. He thrashed, fangs flipping out, as the creatures buried him. A rodent clamped his teeth around his neck. Samael stabbed him until he released him. Lola seized him, mouth digging into his stomach.

More vermin piled on top of the defenseless snake, his tail whipping at them. Rake clutched his body, dragging him away from the wave of vermin. Cradling his head for a moment, their eyes met.

Samael, battered and broken, searched Rake's eyes for a semblance of pity. There was none to be had.

I watched as Rake pulled Samael against his mouth, ripping his head off. As Rake devoured the snake's severed head, Samael's twitching body slid to the floor.

The horde descended upon him, beginning to feed.

As they fed, I noticed a hammer left beside one of the living room chairs. I snatched it, skirting out of the room and into the entryway.

I came upon the boarded door and began my work. With the hammer's claw, I dragged out one of the nails. Then another. And another.

As I pulled one of the wooden planks from the door, a cockroach slammed into me. Legs wrapped around my body while antennas searched me. I swung the hammer at the insect, smashing its head until it cracked open.

The cockroach released me, crumpling to the ground. Dead.

I resumed my labor. After dragging each nail out, I pulled the final wooden plank from the door. Flinging it open, the hallway stretched before me.

Suddenly, a lizard charged at me. Leaping out of the way, the creature flew through the open door and disappeared down the corridor.

Satisfied with my work, I limped from the entryway and traipsed back through the living room where the pack remained, swarming and feeding on bits of Samael's headless body.

I tried to head for the nursery, but Rake blocked my path. Avoiding him, I retreated and stumbled into my bedroom. I pulled the wooden plank from the wall, revealing the secret passageway.

Rake burst through the open doorway, other animals following him.

Without hesitation, I ducked into the secret corridor and dragged the board shut. Pushing myself forward, I crawled on my stomach down the sewage-flooded corridor. Through the walls, I could hear Rake calling to his followers.

"Find the fucking cunt," he shouted to them.

I heard the animals rip the wooden board from the wall.

Bodies tangled in chaos as creatures flooded the passageway. Rake pushed past them, scurrying after me.

I slithered down the passage until I was beside the giant hole in the paneling. I stopped, my nose mere inches away from the wooden spear splintered from the torn ledger. Turning, I saw Rake closing in on me. My hands pressed down.

A reminder: the loose floorboard.

Rake sprinted toward me; his fangs were exposed.

I pushed the floorboard aside and dove out of his path, dropping into the small chute below.

Rake careened forward, his body slamming into the wooden spear. I covered my head, a vulgar thud above me.

Then, silence.

Climbing out of the crawlspace, I found Rake's limbs dangling there and without movement. His head impaled. Fluid drooled from his open mouth. Light dimmed from his eyes.

The pack of vermin appeared, stampeding the corpse of their slaughtered leader.

I crawled out of the hole, dragging myself into the living room—an empty wreck. Half-eaten body parts bobbed in the sewage. The walls were slimed with blood and excrement.

Carrying the hammer, I limped down the corridor until I reached the nursery.

I went to the crawlspace hidden behind the leaking sewer pipe. The newborn stirred in his blanket, wailing at me.

I could hear claws scurrying down the hallway. The squeal of rodents as they approached.

"She went this way," one of them shouted.

"Get the bitch!"

I eyed the sewage pipe. I followed the large tube until it disappeared into the split wall, a giant crack snaking across the room's ceiling.

I made the decision.

Slamming the hammer against the pipe, the duct shifted and groaned.

I gripped the handle, striking once again. More sewage spilled into the room, the pipe listing. The ceiling split further with creaks. Water dripped through the open cracks. I looked up from my work, noticing the horde of vermin in the nursery's doorway.

One last strike: I slammed the hammer down. Dragged the giant pipe out of the wall.

The ceiling cracked open, the pipe crashing into the floor. I watched as the valve shattered, releasing a flood of sewage water into the room. The horde retreated, a wave of water hurtling toward them.

I clawed at the drywall with my hammer, pushing myself inside the crawlspace until I was covered.

The ceiling burst open, a giant shelf crashing and burying me and the child inside the crawlspace. I watched as another sewage pipe plunged down, water roaring through the room like whitewater rapids.

The flood of the apocalypse.

Sewage water blasted through the apartment, bodies tossing against the current. Another surge of water thundered, walls ripping open as if they were merely sheets of paper. A massive wave crashed into the room, carrying vermin through the open entryway and down the corridor until they disappeared.

Crouching behind a ledger, I pulled the crying newborn tight against me and waited for it to be over.

CHAPTER SIXTEEN

I PEERED OUT from the hole in the crawlspace when it was quiet again. The walls dripped glimmering beads of water as if the apartment were a dredged sunken ship.

I watched as soldiers in black tactical gear and gas masks stormed the apartment. Guns drawn and aimed, they scanned the room for signs of life.

I watched as a soldier discovered a woman's body curled in the corner. He flipped her over. Dead. Her right arm was tattooed with an emerald sleeve of scales like a lizard. Parts of her face and hands had been eaten away.

I heard a voice call to the men from outside the room.

"Status report," the voice ordered.

"I've got another," the soldier reported, leaning the woman's corpse against the wall.

The voice counted off. "Seven."

I watched as one of the soldiers peered through an opening in one of the panels, his flashlight searching the secret passageway. I followed the light until it arrived at a dark figure slumped forward as if praying at the end of the secret corridor.

Flashlight searching the dead man's body: a pair of black goggles were strapped to his head and glimmered like the eyes of an insect. Dressed entirely in black, the figure faced away from the soldier and leaned against a post. Limbs were sprawled and without movement, his throat speared with a giant wooden splinter.

"Eight," the soldier reported.

I watched as the soldier moved back into the nursery. He was about to leave when the newborn in my arm began to fuss, mewling.

He turned, aiming his gun as if expecting the worst. He skirted through the debris, lifting chunks of ceiling plaster and exposing the wall's hollow pocket. He peered inside the crawlspace, and I greeted him.

The baby stirred, shrieking, as it shifted beneath the blanket.

"Sergeant," he shouted, "I've got two civilians here."

The soldier pointed a flashlight at me, the light finding my severed arm and blood hosing my stomach.

"I need a medic," he shouted.

I lifted my head, eyelids threatening to close as he held out an arm for me to grab.

"I've got you," he said.

I remained unmoving. I squinted, the shouts of my rescuer dimming to silence. Light began to shimmer all around me, swallowing me until I could feel nothing.

I awakened later, and found I had been moved out from inside the crawlspace and onto the nursery's mattress. My arm had been wrapped with bandages and a tourniquet.

A medic swathed my forehead with dressings. I flinched, unsure, at the tenderness of his touch. A sergeant moved beside me, removing his gas mask.

"We're going to move you now," he told me.

I winced, eyes closing, as the medic slid my body onto a nearby folding stretcher.

I watched as a soldier, shifting in the room's corner, aimed his flashlight behind a small wooden board leaning against the wall. His fingers pulled at sheets of crumpled paper stuffed behind the ledger. Finally, he pulled out the small leather-bound journal.

Opening the small journal, he leafed through every page. I watched his eyes widen as he looked. I knew exactly what he saw—page after page filled with chicken scratch. The margins decorated with ornate drawings of insects and other kinds of vermin as circus performers. A lizard breathing fire. A spider balancing on a trapeze.

Just then, another soldier entered the room.

"Clear, sir," he reported.

"Let's move," the sergeant ordered.

I lifted my head, noticing the blanket-swaddled newborn hugging the soldier's chest.

"Please," I begged him. "May I hold him?"

The soldier looked to the sergeant for direction. The sergeant merely nodded: "Go ahead."

Leaning over me, he slid the infant into my arm. I pulled the precious bundle tight against my side, his bald, pink head resting on my stomach.

The medic and soldier lifted both ends of the stretcher, carrying me and the child out of the nursery and into the living room.

They dodged debris, skirting around the massive ledge of collapsed ceiling.

I pulled the newborn close against me. "Happy birthday," I said to him.

I pressed my chapped lips against him as he squirmed. "This story is called 'Lament for a Lost Unicorn,'" I told him. "Once, there was a beautiful unicorn a blind man and his wife found."

I didn't notice as the soldiers carried me over the threshold and finally out of the apartment—the disaster zone.

"One night, someone broke into the stable and tried to steal it," I told the infant as the soldiers continued to carry us down the empty corridor.

"Even though he was able to rescue it, he knew others would come and do worse," I said, the world around me blurring as my eyes remained fixed on the child. "So, he tore off the reins and walked the animal to the edge of the woods."

Carrying us down a flight of stairs, the soldiers ducked beneath a battered doorway ripped off its hinges and finally moved outside.

The street was flooded with sewage. Curtains of fire devoured the charred remnants of neighboring buildings. I heard the distant thunder of bombs exploding, the rattle of gunfire.

I sensed myself loosen, sunlight washing me as the soldiers carried us toward a large armored vehicle idling in the center of the road.

"And he said, 'You'll be hurt if you stay here,'" I told the newborn. "'So,' he said, 'I'm getting you out of here. So you'll never be hurt by anyone ever again.'"

The infant stirred slightly. I kissed him.

Glancing up at the sky, ash-like specks circled in the air and buried us in a blanket of white.

I hugged the child tighter with a promise I knew I would always keep.

ACKNOWLEDGMENTS

MY HEARTFELT GRATITUDE belongs to Scarlett R. Algee (Editor Extraordinaire/the beating heart of JournalStone/Trepidatio) for believing in my manuscript and working so diligently on making it look presentable to the world.

Also, thank you to Sean Leonard for proofreading and working on the manuscript as well.

My eternal thankfulness for my literary agent, Priya Doraswamy, for always encouraging me.

Huge thanks to my Film/TV manager, Ryan Lewis of Spin a Black Yarn, for his endless support and friendship.

Thank you to David Demchuk, Gretchen Felker-Martin, Kathe Koja, and Paul Tremblay for reading the manuscript early and providing stellar endorsements.

Most importantly, thank you to my beloved Ali for reading every word I write (even the not very good ones) and protecting me from the haters. I love you with all my soul.

ABOUT THE AUTHOR

Eric LaRocca (*he/they*) is the Bram Stoker Award nominated author of several works of horror and dark fiction, including the viral sensation, *Things Have Gotten Worse Since We Last Spoke*. A lover of luxury fashion and an admirer of European musical theatre, Eric can often be found roaming the streets of his home city Boston, MA for inspiration. For more information, please follow @hystericteeth on Twitter/Instagram or visit ericlarocca.com.

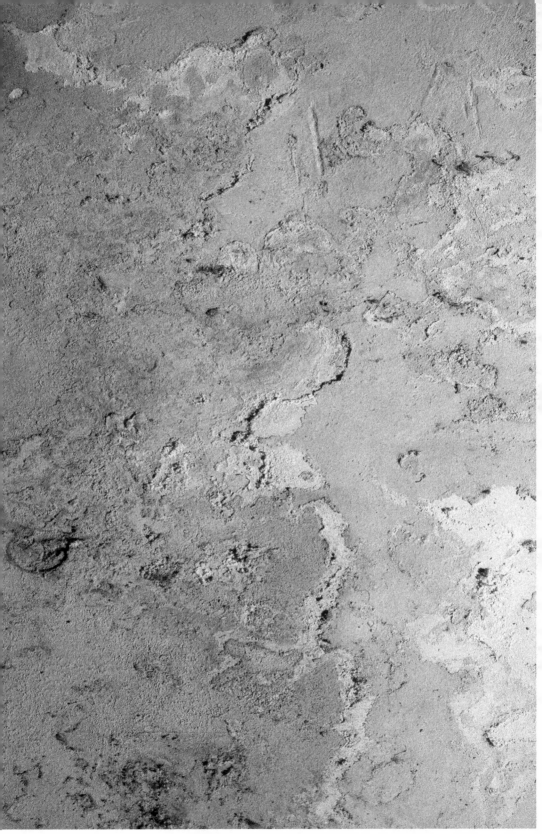